The Phantom of
Tiger Mountain

The Phantom of Tiger Mountain

BY LENSEY NAMIOKA

ILLUSTRATIONS BY ROSS LEWIS

The Vanguard Press

New York

Library of Congress Cataloging-in-Publication Data

Namioka, Lensey.
The phantom of tiger mountain.

Summary: Sightings of a phantom figure occur at the
same time that suspicions of a traitor infiltrate a band of outlaws, dropouts
from more respectable
sectors of Chinese society, now living by their wits
during the Song dynasty.
[1. Robbers and outlaws—Fiction. 2. China—History
—Song Dynasty, 960-1279—Fiction] I. Title.
PZ7.N1426Ph 1986   [Fic]   85-26314
ISBN 0-8149-0912-4
Designer: Kay Lee
Manufactured in the United States of America.

The Phantom of
Tiger Mountain

1

The Phantom in White

The chieftain was out of sight. Little Li put the money box down on a flat boulder, pulled off his scarf and wiped his face. He was called Little Li because he was the youngest of the outlaw band, although in size he was the biggest. That was why he had been assigned to carry the heavy money box when the band escaped into the hills after the raid.

Wu Meng and his father, Old Wu, were behind, holding off pursuers. Among the outlaws of the Tiger Mountain band, Wu Meng was recognized by everyone as the most skillful fighter, and he always brought up the rear during their raids. The chieftain, of course, couldn't be risked for any dangerous rearguard action, since the welfare of the whole band depended on his safety. He was a wily old fox, a good strategist and tactician, and the raids he planned rarely failed.

Little Li strained his ears but could not hear the chieftain's steps ahead of him. The old fox moved fast and was probably halfway home already. Little Li decided that he was safe from pursuit, and he could afford to take a few moments for a bite to eat. At eighteen he was still growing, and he was always hungry. Tucked in the wide sash that pressed closed the overlapping front of his jacket was a small packet of food wrapped in oiled paper. Little Li pulled out the packet, opened it with a sigh of pleasure, and sat down on the boulder to eat.

The packet contained two flat breads, made of sheets of dough, first sprinkled with chopped onions, then coiled, rolled flat, and baked brown on both sides. For Little Li an even greater treat was the pickled garlic, four precious cloves marinated in vinegar. He was a northerner and found it hard to do without his garlic. He knew that others in the band, mostly local Anhui men, complained about his garlic behind his back, but few of them complained to his face because they were afraid of his long, muscular arms. He didn't even have to lay a finger on them: he could blow them down with his breath.

The moon was half full. The chieftain had timed the raid so that the night would be bright enough for the four outlaws to see, but not bright enough for the governor's soldiers to come after them in the mountains. A wisp of cloud passed over the moon and the night darkened. In the wooded hillside, the shadows looked like puddles of ink. Except for the occasional rustle of scrub bamboo made by a passing hare or badger, all was quiet. The chieftain must have gone on far ahead, and there was no sign of the Wus, father and son. Perhaps they had taken the longer route home.

Little Li munched contentedly on his bread. He was

enjoying the peace, which was a pleasant change from the noise and congestion of the outlaw camp. At the beginning of fall, the band had moved to some mountain caves where they would spend the winter. Little Li disliked the jostling in the caves. He was constantly bumping into someone, maybe because he was growing so fast that he couldn't get used to his ever-changing size. And since he was the youngest, he always had to do the apologizing.

When the last of his food was gone, some of his contentment went as well. He felt hemmed in as he often did in the mountains. Little Li's home was in the wide plains of the Yellow River in northern China. After the region had been overrun by Tartars, he had joined a band of deserters, remnants of an imperial army that had been crushed by the barbarians. These former soldiers formed the core of the outlaw band that eventually established itself near Tiger Mountain in the central province of Anhui. Most local people still avoided the mountain, although in living memory no tigers had ever been seen there.

Little Li licked the bread crumbs from his greasy fingers and wiped them on his pants. It was time to be moving again. The chieftain was probably back at the camp, impatient to open the money box and count the loot. Just as Little Li bent down to lift the box, he stiffened.

The stillness was broken by a laugh.

Little Li felt the short hairs rise on the back of his neck as the laughter went on and on. It sounded like a man's laugh, starting with a hoarse, low note that was surely too deep for a woman. But the gust of laughter rose in pitch until it became a giggle. In that shrill giggle was a touch of madness.

Who could it be? Wu Meng, always in complete control of himself, would never break down like this. Old Wu, his father, was the wise and canny adviser to the chieftain, and the sanest man in the band. Lord Heaven! Could it be the chieftain himself? Little Li remembered that the chieftain had been unusually nervous lately. He jumped at any sudden noise, and changed color for no apparent reason. Perhaps the responsibilities of leadership were weighing on him. Times had been lean recently, and the band was growing unmanageable.

Little Li jumped to his feet. He had to find his leader, and quickly. Just as he turned toward the direction taken by the chieftain, something white caught the corner of his eye. He whirled around. As he did, the moon came out from behind a thin layer of cloud, and in its cold light Little Li saw clearly a slender figure dressed in white. It threw back its head and gave a bellow of laughter that rose to the same unsettling giggle. Then the figure turned abruptly and plunged behind some pine trees.

Cursing, Little Li jumped forward in pursuit. At least he knew now that this was not his leader breaking down into hysteria. This was some prankster trying to frighten him. He could think of several people in the outlaw band who were capable of such mischief, Gao San for instance, and a few of his friends.

But before he could go far, Little Li heard a groan coming from the hill above him. Looking up into a small clearing, he saw the chieftain crouched on the ground, covering his face with his hands. Little Li's heart thumped with alarm as he raced up to his leader. "Did he hurt you, sir?" he cried.

The chieftain slowly raised his head. "Who?" He spoke with a struggle and his speech was slurred.

"The man in white just now," said Little Li. He knelt down beside his leader and looked at him anxiously, trying to see if there was a wound.

An unexpected expression came over the chieftain's face. Little Li realized that it was relief, relief mixed with something else. Calculation?

"Then you saw it too?" asked the chieftain. He still sounded stunned, but his voice was slightly stronger.

"I could hardly miss it, sir," said Little Li. "The moon came out just then. And I heard it. It was laughing like a maniac."

"Yes," murmured the chieftain. "So it was." After a moment he rose. "We should be moving. Old Wu and his son may be back already and wondering what's happening to us."

Little Li stood up, towering over the slight figure of the chieftain. "Are you sure you're not hurt, sir?" he asked again. "You can lean on me for support."

"No, I'm not hurt," said the chieftain testily. His voice had regained its normal crispness. "I was just startled." He suddenly turned sharply. "Where did you leave the money box?"

"It's . . . it's down there, on a boulder." Little Li was embarrassed that he had forgotten about the loot, the purpose of all these weeks of planning, hard work, and risks. "I'll go and . . ."

He was interrupted by the sound of voices coming from below. He recognized Wu Meng's voice and it seemed that the Wus had finally caught up with them.

But when the young fighter came into sight, Little Li saw that he was not accompanied by Old Wu. The man he had with him—that he dragged, rather—was a stranger. When Wu Meng saw the chieftain, he gave his captive a hard push that sent him sprawling.

The chieftain instantly became the efficient, businesslike leader. "Good. I see you got safely away from the soldiers. What do you have here?"

Wu Meng bowed briefly to his chief. "I caught this fellow sneaking behind me. He's probably a spy. Do we have any use for him, or do we kill him?"

The chieftain looked thoughtfully at the stranger. "Hm . . . let's question him first."

The stranger climbed to his feet. "I am most certainly not a spy," he said, drawing himself up haughtily. His dignity was marred by a cut lip still oozing blood. "This warrior here did not offer me an opportunity to explain myself before he dealt me a blow that rendered speech temporarily difficult."

Little Li stared, fascinated. He had never before met anyone who spoke so fluently and used such high-flown expressions. Most of the outlaws spoke in grunts.

The chieftain's mustache twitched. "Very well. Explain yourself."

The stranger dusted and straightened his clothes before replying. "Your outlaw band here on Tiger Mountain has commanded my admiration for some time," he said, gesturing gracefully at the three outlaws. "Now, certain recent events at home have made it inconvenient for me to continue my normal mode of existence. Extensive education notwithstanding, I found employment opportunities in the city limited. Therefore I have decided to join your band and offer my services."

"What services?" asked Wu Meng, raising his brows. He turned to the chieftain. "We have no use for this skinny bookworm. He'd just be another useless mouth to feed, and a busy mouth at that."

The chieftain stroked his long moustache and wispy beard. "We might have use for an educated man," he said slowly. "Can you write well?" he asked the stranger.

The stranger grinned, lopsidedly because of his cut lip. "My calligraphy is superb! Moreover, I command a variety of writing styles: official documents, belles lettres, poetry, anything you desire. You might find it useful, for example, to be able to send an 'official' message."

The suggestion was interesting. Of the outlaw band, only the chieftain and the two Wus could read and write, and even they would not be able to muster the style required in official documents. The chieftain thought over the idea, and finally a faint smile appeared on his thin, shrewd face. "All right, we'll give you a trial in our band. You can be our scribe."

Even Wu Meng's face relaxed. "Some of our men have left their womenfolk behind," he said, "and sending them some comforting messages would make the separation easier and would improve morale." He turned to the stranger. "Can you write that kind of letter?"

"Tender messages are a specialty of mine," said the stranger, laughing.

Little Li started at the sound of that laughter. He strode

over to the stranger and seized him by the collar. "You were the one who was trying to frighten us just now by laughing like a lunatic!"

The stranger flinched. "Would you mind not breathing in my face? I'm beginning to feel faint."

"Let him go, Little Li," ordered the chieftain. "He's not the one. Look: his clothes are different."

Little Li let go and slowly stepped back. Of course the chieftain was right. The apparition had been wearing white, and this man's jacket and trousers were of some darker material.

"What's this about?" asked Wu Meng. "What happened?"

"Yes, what happened?" asked another voice. Old Wu stepped into the clearing, panting hard.

The chieftain looked at his lieutenant anxiously. "Here, you'd better sit down and rest. Where were you?"

Old Wu sat down heavily, mopping his brow. His hair was straggling loose from its topknot, and even his mous-tache looked ragged. After catching his breath he said, "Some of the soldiers got on my tail, because I was slower than the rest of you, I suppose. It took a bit of circling around to lose them."

"I'm sorry, old friend," the chieftain said gently. "You shouldn't even be on these raids. Next time you'd better stay behind. We need you in the camp anyway to keep the hotheads there from getting into trouble."

Old Wu looked up fiercely. "Don't try to pamper me! Just remember that you're a year older than I am, and when I'm too creaky to go on raids, you'll have to be carried on a litter!"

The Phantom of Tiger Mountain • 8

Wu Meng chuckled, and after a moment the chieftain joined in. Little Li felt no amusement. He remembered how shaken his leader had been a short while ago, and he wondered how long the two older men could continue to take an active part in the raids. He himself felt Wu Meng would be a more suitable leader for their strenuous expeditions, but he knew the chieftain was reluctant to admit this.

Old Wu seemed to notice the stranger for the first time. "Who's this?" he demanded.

"Some youngster who got into trouble at home and wants to join our band," said his son.

"Oh? What sort of trouble?" Old Wu asked.

"He didn't tell us and we don't want to know," Wu Meng said quickly. "If you let him open his mouth we'll be here all night. In fact, it's nearly morning already."

"We'd better be going," said the chieftain. He turned to the stranger. "All right, you can come along with us. But remember: you're not officially a member of the Tiger Mountain band until you prove yourself."

The new recruit bowed elaborately. "That is only to be expected. My eternal gratitude for . . ."

"Where's the money?" interrupted Old Wu. "I hope we got as much as our spy said there would be."

"I'll get the money box," said Little Li. He ran down to the flat boulder on which he had left the box. The wooden brass-reinforced box was still on the boulder where he had left it, and he heaved it up to his shoulder.

Plodding after the others, he tried to keep an eye on the new recruit to see if he was up to any tricks. He could hear the chieftain telling Old Wu about the strange figure that had startled them by its eerie laughter. The chieftain was trying to make light of the incident, but Little Li was not deceived. He remembered the terror on his leader's face.

Dawn was approaching when the outlaws reached the narrow pass that led to their secret hideout. The pass was defended by hidden guards poised to ambush any unwanted intruders. The chieftain stopped and twice whistled a bird-call, the cry of a bullfinch. The invisible defenders of the pass recognized the day's signal and responded, and now it was safe for the outlaws to proceed.

Walking in single file, they carefully negotiated the treacherous, winding passage. Little Li found it difficult to watch his feet while carrying the heavy box, but fortunately it was growing light enough for him to see ahead.

At last they came out of the pass and into the long, secluded glen that sheltered the outlaw camp. Where the trees grew thin, yellow limestone could be seen; perhaps there never had been tigers here, and the color of the rocks had given Tiger Mountain its name. One side of the glen was protected by a sheer rocky cliff, and boring into the cliff were half a dozen natural caves—warm, dry, and cozy winter quarters for the outlaw band. Finding the glen had been an extraordinary stroke of luck, for it was a comfortable, wholesome site. It was also defensible against even an army, as long as the secret of the pass was safe.

Despite the hour the camp was already stirring. Nearly all the thirty outlaws in the camp were up, no doubt eagerly waiting to see the result of the raid. As word of the chieftain's return reached them, the men hurried out of their caves. Laughter and cheers broke out when Little Li grinned broadly and held up the money box for all to see.

Now that he had reached the camp and could relax, Little Li could feel sleepiness coming over him, numbing his arms and legs. When he finally set the heavy box down in front of the chieftain's cave, he was so thankful to be rid of his burden that it took him a moment to realize there was something odd about the money box, something he hadn't noticed during their hurried flight back. He couldn't hear a clinking of coins.

Fighting down panic, he placed his hands flat over the box, almost afraid to look inside. "Open it!" the outlaws around him cried. "What are you waiting for?"

Little Li couldn't put off the moment any longer. Slowly he undid the brass clasp and lifted the lid of the money box. It was just as he had feared: the box was filled with rocks.

There was a stunned silence. Then, with a wild cry of rage, Little Li threw himself on the new recruit and seized him by the throat. Dimly he was aware of shouts around him, but he tightened his fingers, intent only on squeezing the life from the foul dog who had stolen their money.

Suddenly powerful hands grasped him by the shoulders and flung him aside. Only one person in the band was strong enough to do that. Little Li looked up and saw Wu Meng standing above him.

"You idiot!" the young fighter snapped. "Do you want to kill him before he tells us where he put the money?"

Little Li hung his head. Once again he had acted without thinking first. When would he learn self-control like Wu Meng's?

By now nearly the whole outlaw band had gathered, and

most of them were growling angrily. Wu Meng turned and glared at them. "Quiet! We want to hear!"

The muttering subsided, although murderous looks were still concentrated on the stranger. The new recruit struggled to his feet, and in the morning light he presented a sorry sight. His lip was bleeding again, and his throat showed livid bruises. He swallowed painfully a few times. "I've arrived at the conclusion that joining the outlaws of Tiger Mountain is not one of my more inspired notions," he croaked. He attempted to speak jauntily, but he could not prevent his voice from quavering.

"But I'm afraid it's too late for you to go home again," the chieftain reminded him gently. "You've already seen the secret pass to our hideout. And besides, you have some things to tell us first."

The new recruit closed his eyes for a moment. Then he opened them and sighed. "The only thing I can tell you is that I don't know what happened to the money. Of course you'll have a hard time believing me."

Wu Meng grinned ferociously. "Believe me, you'll be the one who will have a hard time—if you don't tell us where the money is."

A few of the outlaws laughed, but they stopped at a look from Wu Meng. Suddenly the new recruit straightened. "An interesting thought has just occurred to me," he said to Wu Meng. "If I had stolen the money, the sensible action for me would be to rush downhill as speedily as possible. Why should I be so foolish as to follow you into the mountains?"

"Little Li," the chieftain said curtly, "exactly when did you leave the money box unguarded?"

"I had it in my sight constantly until we saw that figure in white," Little Li replied quickly.

"I see," said the chieftain slowly. He turned to Wu Meng. "When did you capture this man?"

Wu Meng scowled. "I caught him at the foot of the hill, soon after I escaped from the soldiers . . . yes . . . I see what you mean now."

The chieftain nodded. "That means you had already caught this man before Little Li left the box behind."

The conclusion was inescapable. The stranger could not have been the one who took the money while the box was left unguarded.

Old Wu laughed without humor. "So what did happen? Is Little Li lying? Or my son? Maybe he and the stranger conspired to steal the money. Or maybe *I* stole the money while you were busy talking to each other in the clearing." His face grew grave. "There is another possibility: the box never contained any money in the first place."

That meant there was a traitor in the camp—someone who had warned the governor of the intended raid. The money box could have held rocks, not coins, all along.

The chieftain suddenly looked old. "Without proof, all this is just idle speculation," he said heavily. Their funds were running low, and the failure of the raid was a serious blow. Even more serious was the possibility of treachery.

But the chieftain's voice was calm enough as he addressed the new recruit. "Very well, you will join our band as our scribe."

To Little Li he said, "Find him some quarters and show him his duties. It's best if you put him in your cave, where you can keep an eye on him."

2

The New Recruit

Little Li was awakened by the sound of voices in the cave. "Look at the two babies sleeping away! Aren't they sweet?"

It was the hateful voice of Gao San. With his slow northern speech, Little Li was teased mercilessly by the other outlaws. His worst tormentor was Gao San, who lost no opportunity to complain, among other things, about the northerner's garlic breath. Since the two shared a cave, Gao San's opportunities were many.

"No, you're wrong. Little Li is going to be the nursemaid for a change. Didn't you hear the chieftain telling him to take care of the new recruit?"

This was the voice of Gao San's shadow, who was called the butcher because that had been his former occupation. The two men were inseparable, and at least once a day their barbed comments drove Little Li to fury. Since his fists were faster than his tongue, he usually found himself being reprimanded by Wu Meng for starting a fight. This morning Little Li resolved to keep his temper. Of course he always made that resolution.

Opening his eyes, he looked toward the mouth of the cave and saw to his surprise that the sun was high. He had meant to snatch only a brief rest, but it seemed he had slept till nearly noon.

He sat up quickly and, ignoring the grinning faces of Gao San and the butcher, turned to look at the new recruit.

The new scribe was sleeping soundly, totally exhausted by his night's activities. Looking at the sleeping face, Little Li suddenly realized that the man was younger than he had thought, perhaps only a couple of years older than himself. Little Li shook him, none too gently.

The scribe groaned. "Tell the cook not to hold breakfast for me," he muttered. "I want to sleep some more."

Gao San and the butcher guffawed, their laughter bouncing off the walls of the deep, narrow cave. At the sound, the scribe opened his eyes. He propped himself up on one elbow and slowly looked around the cave, taking in the rough limestone walls, the niches holding household utensils, the floor of yellow dirt. His eyes finally came to the three outlaws.

"It's not a dream," he said slowly. "I really did it. I joined the outlaws of Tiger Mountain!"

"Now that you've joined us, you'd better get up," growled Little Li. "There's work to be done."

The scribe sat up and stretched. "My appetite is unusually keen for this hour of the day. It must be the consequence of all that unaccustomed exercise last night. Where is the dining hall?"

"'Where is the dining hall?'" said Gao San, mimicking

the genteel tone of the scribe, and he roared with laughter again. "His appetite is unusually keen!"

"It must be all that unaccustomed exercise!" shrieked the butcher, nearly doubled over with laughter.

The scribe raised his brows and studied the two red-faced outlaws. His eyes rested on Gao San's paunch. "There seems to be a good supply of pig's bladder here," he murmured. "If the chieftain ever plans a raid across water, he can inflate a couple of these bladders and use them as floats."

It took a second for the insult to reach home. Gao San's laughter choked to a stop. Then he sprang toward the scribe. "Why, you—"

Little Li's long, muscular arm shot out and hooked Gao San's neck. "Now, now, calm down. Remember what Wu Meng told us about fighting." It gave him immense satisfaction to say this. Normally *he* was the one to receive such a warning.

Gao San struggled without success against Little Li's powerful arm and soon became quiet. "All right," he muttered. Turning to the butcher, he said, "Come on. We have better things to do than squabble here."

Little Li felt a warm sense of fellowship spread over him as he turned to the new recruit. With his muscles and the scribe's sharp tongue, the two of them could make a formidable team. But the warmth was short-lived.

The scribe pushed back his bedclothes and stood up. "Can you tell the girls to heat some bath water?" he said. "I feel incredibly grubby, and I should like to bathe myself before eating my breakfast."

Little Li took a deep breath. "Listen," he informed his charge, "you are not on a picnic in the mountains to view a scenic waterfall. You are with a band of outlaws, and you have to live like an outlaw. There are no girls to heat bath water for you. Not only do you have to carry your own water from the stream, you have to bring water for others in the camp, and that is your first assigned duty for the day."

It was the longest speech Little Li had ever made in his life. Perhaps he was feeling the influence of the new recruit.

For once the scribe was speechless. When he found his voice again, he sounded hollow. "Do you mean there are no women in this camp? We have to do our own cooking and cleaning?"

"There are only half a dozen women here altogether," Little Li told him, "and they serve the senior officers. Low-ranking men like us have to do everything ourselves."

"But I don't know how to cook!" wailed the scribe.

"I'll have to teach you," Little Li said without enthusiasm. Then, seeing the other man's dismay, he said, "That can wait. Right now you can share some of my onion bread. I still have some left from yesterday." He rose and fetched a package of his bread from the niche above his head. He had made a dozen of the flat breads the day before, hoping they would last him for a couple of days.

The scribe looked at the breads suspiciously. Like most Anhui people, he preferred rice. But when he ate a mouthful of the bread, he looked up in surprise. "This tastes better than I anticipated. Perhaps the vile reputation of northern cuisine is undeserved."

Little Li nodded. "When you're hungry, everything tastes good."

As the scribe ate, he looked at the crude furnishings in

the cave: beds made of planks resting on wooden frames lashed together with twine, wooden stools still showing the marks of the ax, much-mended cotton quilts on the beds. "I can see that the place lacks a woman's touch," he remarked. "How can your band get by with only half a dozen women? And don't the men fight over them?"

"We visit nearby villages when we want female company," muttered Little Li, blushing. "The country folk around here have an understanding with us, and we have many friends in the villages."

"Oho, so that's the way of it," said the scribe thoughtfully. "And I suppose your friends also supply you with a certain amount of information?"

"Yes, in fact we have someone who . . ." Little Li stopped himself. There was no need to mention the spy the outlaws had in the governor's mansion. The scribe was still on probation here, and it would not be wise to trust him with such secrets.

Little Li started on his second bread and remembered to offer another one to his guest. He was sorry when his offer was accepted. At this rate his supply wouldn't last long.

The scribe chewed vigorously. "Some green tea would go well with this bread—not too strong, but plenty of it."

"We don't have time to boil water for tea," Little Li told him. "If you're thirsty, you can drink cold water. And that reminds me, I'll show you where the stream is. You'd better get started on your work."

"You're serious?" said the scribe. "You really mean I have to carry water?"

"Stop wasting time," Little Li said curtly. "Take those two jars over there."

They walked through the camp, which was bustling with its normal midday activities. In a large clearing Wu Meng was instructing four men in the art of fencing with wooden sticks. In front of the largest cave, the chieftain and Old Wu were sitting with their heads together, talking earnestly. One outlaw was fanning a fire for cooking his noonday rice, while another man was unloading a bundle of twigs he had gathered for firewood.

The scribe gazed around him wide-eyed with wonder, and Little Li had to prod him forward. At the stream, Little Li explained the scribe's duties. "We have six caves here, and each one has a large crock that holds eight jars of water for drinking, cooking, washing, and so on. It's your work to fill those water jars."

The scribe's jaw dropped. "But that means I have to carry forty-eight jars of water! I have to make twenty-four trips altogether!"

Little Li grinned. "Such fast work with numbers! It must be all that education." As he walked off he said, "Call me when you're through. I'll be practicing kung fu over there in that glade."

The kung fu instructor was a bull-necked defrocked monk with a scratchy voice. He had joined the Tiger Mountain band because, he said, he had become tired of chanting sutras. His hoarseness, he claimed, came from inhaling too much incense. Nobody even pretended to believe his story, but neither did anyone question him about his true reasons for leaving his monastery. The outlaws made it a practice not to question one another too closely about their backgrounds.

Normally, Little Li enjoyed the kung fu sessions, but

today he could not quite get his mind away from the scribe. The chieftain, after all, had told him to watch the man. Out of the corner of his eye Little Li saw the scribe repeatedly toil up the hill with his wooden jars. Between trips he rested, and the rests grew longer and longer.

With his attention only half on his practice, Little Li received a blow that winded him. His opponent was the butcher, who had never before bested him in kung fu.

"You're not paying attention," the monk told Little Li. "Go away and don't come back until you can concentrate."

Dusting himself off, Little Li walked back to his cave. He found the scribe sprawled in front, looking dejectedly at his hands.

"Finished already?" Little Li asked him.

The scribe groaned. "Finished? I'm not even halfway done. So far I've carried only twenty pails!"

"You don't have to hurry," Little Li said cheerfully. "There's plenty of time."

"Yes, but look at my blisters," moaned the scribe. He held out his hands, the slender, pampered hands of the educated class. The palms were red and puffed with blisters. "How can you expect me to use a writing brush if my hands are crippled?"

Little Li laughed. "They're not crippled! Don't worry, after a few days you'll get calluses."

"I might not live that long," muttered the scribe. Perhaps he was genuinely worried about his chances of survival. With his fastidious manners, he looked as incongruous in the outlaw camp as a dish of poached quail eggs on a peasant's table.

"Why did you decide to join our band here in Tiger Mountain?" Little Li asked. "With your background, you could have taken the civil examinations to become an official."

"I did take the examinations," admitted the scribe.

"And you failed them?" asked Little Li. That superb calligraphy, that command of writing styles, and that torrential fluency had not been enough after all, he thought.

The scribe grimaced. "I failed the examinations because I couldn't resist the temptation to write some bawdy verses in the answer to one of the questions."

"You can't mean it!" cried Little Li, appalled.

"I suppose not," said the scribe lightly. But for an instant a shadow passed over his face and he looked so forlorn that Little Li was touched. "All right, I'll carry the rest of the water for you," he said gruffly. "But that's just for today."

"Thank you," said the scribe, so quickly that it sounded as if he had been waiting for the offer.

As Little Li filled the remaining water jars one by one, he had the feeling that he had been tricked.

The soft yellow light of the dish lamp was kind to their wrinkles, thought the chieftain. Old Wu looked twenty years younger, and he himself probably looked as he had in his prime. Or maybe not. His wrinkles went much deeper than those of his friend, and they could not be softened even by the lamplight.

He heard the churring call of a thrush in the trees outside the cave, and the sound reminded him of the many nights he used to spend outside his house after dinner. His mind was always clearest at this time of night, and his best ideas came to him as he sat listening to the soft, busy sounds of animals and birds.

Meimei, his serving girl, poured more hot water over the tea leaves in their cups. As always, her hands moved deftly. Although she said her family had been shopkeepers, she had the refinement of a girl from a more affluent background. Perhaps she had served in the family store and had learned the manners of her upper-class customers. Meimei said little about her family, and the chieftain knew only that her mother was sickly and that Meimei had found living under the same roof with her brother and his wife a strain.

If his wife had been alive, thought the chieftain, he could take Meimei as a secondary wife. Since his wife had died, however, he could not marry Meimei, for that would make her his principal wife, and she had neither the birth nor the money for such a match. Outlaw that he was, the chieftain had once been General Han Baota of the Imperial Song Army, and a Han could not ally himself with Meimei's lowly family.

Reluctantly the chieftain took his eyes from Meimei and turned to his old friend. "What do you think the Tartars are doing now?" he asked.

Old Wu drank his tea in slow slurps, inhaling the fragrant steam. "The Tartars? They're probably consolidating their hold on the north," he said.

"They won't be satisfied with only half the country," Wu Meng said. "Unless we do something, within a few years they'll sweep over the whole of China."

"What do you expect us to do that we haven't done

already?" Old Wu asked bitterly. "It's hopeless, I tell you. The Song dynasty is finished."

"I'm not so sure," said the chieftain. "The south is holding, and that's where the capital is—the government at Hangzhou looks stable enough. Certainly the artists, poets, and craftsmen are working away with no worries about tomorrow."

"And what will the emperor do when a Tartar general knocks at the gate of Hangzhou?" demanded Old Wu. "Spout poetry at him?"

"Instead of painters and poets, we need some good soldiers!" said Wu Meng.

The chieftain's smile was wry. "Good soldiers aren't enough. In our last campaign, our soldiers were as good as they had ever been, but they weren't issued their weapons in time because of a 'misunderstanding' with the quartermaster—'misunderstanding' meaning that I wasn't able to give him a large enough bribe. No wonder we were beaten."

"We were beaten because our troops were no match for those wild Tartar horsemen," Old Wu said bluntly.

"If the Tartars can train horsemen, so can we," insisted Wu Meng. "People are beginning to think the Tartars can't be stopped. We have to prove they're wrong."

"And you, personally, will train enough horsemen to stem the barbarian horde?" asked the chieftain. Instantly he regretted his sarcasm. He knew he was envious of the younger man's fire.

Wu Meng's hands briefly tightened around his teacup, then immediately he had his temper under control. "I will not live to see my country ruled by barbarians," he said quietly.

"Will it really make a difference to the peasants," asked the chieftain, "whether they are being ruled by the Tartars or by our own corrupt officials?"

"It will make a difference to me," said Wu Meng.

The chieftain sighed. "Are you proposing we lead the Tiger Mountain band against the Tartars?"

"Just that," said Wu Meng. "This band can be the nucleus of a new army. We have supporters among the people, and we can attract more men."

In spite of himself, the chieftain was stirred. "General Han Baota returns from the dead," he murmured. Then he shook his head. "It will never work. I'll be accused of desertion for having abandoned the army after our disastrous defeat four years ago. Some people at court might even demand my arrest for treason."

"Not if you win a battle against the Tartars first," Wu Meng pointed out. "They can't arrest a winning general."

"Oh, can't they?" said the chieftain. "You're forgetting General Yue Fei, who had won a string of spectacular victories. But that didn't keep him from being murdered by jealous courtiers."

There was no answer to that, the chieftain knew. The Song dynasty had started gloriously but like so many other dynasties before it, it had been weakened by court intrigue. Ambitious eunuchs and imperial consorts struggled endlessly for power, ignoring the threat of barbarians from the north. The court tried repeatedly to bribe the barbarian leaders, or to play one against another. The Tartar tribe now occupying the northern half of the country had been actually invited by a former emperor as a counter against another barbarian tribe.

When Meimei finished pouring the last of the hot water, she retired to the back of the cave, which was screened off by a cloth hanging to form the chieftain's sleeping quarters. The three men continued to sit and chat idly, discussing how they could defeat the barbarians, given the weapons and men they needed. It was a game they often played, a nostalgic look at the past when the chieftain had been General Han Baota of the Imperial Song Army and Old Wu one of his most trusted captains.

"This is just like the old days," sighed Old Wu. "Remember how the three of us used to map our strategy and then plan where we were going to place our troops?"

At these words the chieftain was pierced by a sharp pang. It was true that three men used to plan the campaigns, the chieftain, Old Wu, and one other. But the third man had not been Wu Meng, then a youngster barely twenty. No, the third man of the inseparable trio had been Zhang Ru.

The chieftain flinched from the thought of Zhang Ru. To change the subject he said, "What do you think of our new recruit?"

Old Wu sniffed. "A spoiled idler from some well-to-do family. What possible use can you find for someone like that?"

"I can think of a number of occasions when we can use someone who looks gentlemanly and respectable," said Wu Meng. "The trouble is, I don't really trust him. There's something about him that doesn't seem quite right."

"What's that?" asked the chieftain.

"Well, he wasn't frightened enough," replied Wu Meng.

"He was frightened, all right," said the chieftain. "When the money box was opened and found to be full of rocks, he was badly frightened, I could tell. But that doesn't mean he took the money. The timetable proves he couldn't have. Don't worry, I'll find a use for him."

Old Wu yawned and stood up. "Then I hope you find a way of using his talents to replenish our funds. Well, I'm off to bed. I'll let you scheme away, you old fox."

Wu Meng rose as well and wished the chieftain a good rest. After the two men left, the chieftain called his serving girl. Receiving no answer, he rose and pushed aside the cloth hanging. Meimei was already fast asleep on the bed, and in repose she looked young enough to be his daughter. The chieftain sighed.

When Meimei had first joined the band two months before, the chieftain had taken her for his mistress as a matter of course. He was the leader, and he had the right of first choice. Only later did he suspect that Wu Meng was attracted to her. The younger man had said nothing, done nothing, but his eyes were often on Meimei, and he always looked away quickly when he saw the chieftain observing him.

Did Meimei like Wu Meng? The chieftain could not tell. She was intelligent as well as beautiful, but she gave away very little of her true feelings. Certainly she showed no sign of discontent in serving him. He believed she was even proud of her status as his serving girl.

Looking around the silent cave, the chieftain felt again the loneliness of leadership, a loneliness emphasized by his usual wakefulness long after the rest of the outlaw band were fast asleep.

On an impulse he rose and went outside, hoping to find Old Wu or one of the others still awake. But as he walked past the entrances of the other caves, all he could hear were the sonorous snores of men exhausted after a strenuous day.

Above the camp was a waterfall, and he had often found the sound of the splashing water soothing. Perhaps he could sit there for a few minutes of peace, and sleep would then come more easily.

In the moonlight the thin waterfall looked like threads of silver. The chieftain sat near it and let the sound of the water work its usual magic. His mind was busy again with plans to improve the fortunes of his band. Already he had glimmers of an idea, a plan that would serve a double purpose. . . .

Soon, chilled by the dampness from the fine spray of the waterfall, the chieftain began to shiver. Now that it was autumn, he really should be wearing warmer clothing. Old Wu had sensibly given in to the weather and started to wear a heavier, lined jacket. But he himself, like a stubborn fool, was still wearing the thin unlined jacket worn by the younger men of the band, because he wanted to show them that he was just as robust as they. Of course he wasn't. A twinge from his arthritic left knee told him he was too old for midnight strolls in the mountains.

Suddenly he was overcome by a sense of futility. After four years of constant struggling, his outlaw band was barely surviving. In fairness to his men, he should resign and give way to a younger man.

He shivered again, but this time not from the cold. His hands grew cold and clammy, and his heart began to pound. He knew, without a doubt, that the phantom in white had come again. Slowly he forced his eyes up, to gaze on the shadowy figure standing on the other side of the waterfall.

The laughter he heard was softer this time, but it rose to the same shrill giggle. He recognized the sound, of course. How could he ever forget it?

He remembered the scene vividly. He was shouting orders at Zhang Ru, but instead of obeying, the other man hunched over, his shoulders shaking violently. He thought at first that Zhang Ru had been wounded. Then he heard the shrill laughter. The other man's mind had broken under the stress, and he was mad.

Now, by the waterfall, the shrill laughter went on and on, and the chieftain began to wonder if he had gone mad himself. Otherwise how could he hear Zhang Ru's laughter night after night, when his old friend had been dead for more than four years?

The figure veered suddenly and disappeared. Freed from the spell of that unnerving laughter, the chieftain's mind began to work once more. No, he was not mad, for Little Li had also heard the laughter and had seen the eerie figure in white.

As the chieftain slowly walked back to his cave, another possibility struck him like a cold knife through the chest: was Zhang Ru's ghost coming for revenge?

3

Plans for a Daring Raid

When the scribe dropped his stick for the third time, Wu Meng lost his temper. "You idiot!" he roared. "How can I teach you to fence if you can't even hang on to the wooden stick?"

"My blisters are painful," complained the scribe. "They prevent me from maintaining a good grip."

Wu Meng stared. "If you're bothered by a little thing like a blister, what are you going to do when some soldier thrusts a spear into your chest? And that's going to happen on your very first raid if you don't learn to defend yourself!"

"Raid? Defend myself?" The scribe's voice became squeaky. "I wasn't expecting to do anything violent! I thought you wanted me to write letters and things!"

Wu Meng turned to Little Li in disgust. "Take him over to the monk for some kung fu lessons. If his hands are too tender for holding weapons, he'd better learn unarmed combat."

Little Li hurried to obey. Wu Meng rarely lost his temper,

but when he did he was terrifying. Little Li was glad to scuttle out of his sight.

"If you had wrapped some cloths around your hands, you wouldn't have disgraced yourself like that," he said to the new recruit. "It's an honor to receive a lesson from Wu Meng. He's a great warrior, and he used to be a weapons instructor in the Imperial Army."

The scribe sniffed. "I wasn't expecting to become an active combatant when I joined. A wooden stick would be useless in any case against a soldier wielding a spear."

"Not when the stick is in Wu Meng's hands," Little Li said. "You should see him in action!"

"That is not something I look forward to with enthusiasm," the scribe said sourly.

The monk surveyed his new student thoughtfully. "Hm . . . well, at least you have the right build—no extra fat to slow you down. And you have a long reach, I see. But more important than a good build is a good attitude. Let's see if you have that."

It was quickly apparent that the scribe did not have a good attitude. The monk threw his new student all over the clearing and soon grew bored with the exercise. "I have better things to do," he snorted, and he stalked off to instruct pupils who were not quite so limp.

Little Li walked over to the scribe, who groaned and sat up, feeling himself all over. By some miracle, he had broken no bones.

"Well, at least you learned how to fall correctly," Little Li said, trying to sound encouraging.

"I don't mind falling," said the scribe. "It's getting up again that I detest."

Little Li heard laughter. He turned and scowled blackly at Gao San, the butcher, and several other grinning outlaws who had been enjoying the spectacle. At a hoarse bellow from the monk, they turned reluctantly and went back to their own practicing.

Since Little Li was officially the guardian of the new recruit, he felt some of the disgrace fall on his own head. "Why don't you even *try* to be a good fighter," he asked, exasperated.

"Why should I?" asked the scribe. "I cannot conceive of a situation in which quick wits and a facile tongue wouldn't serve better than brute strength."

"Are you saying that someone like Wu Meng is a brute?" demanded Little Li.

"I wouldn't presume to say that about your hero," said the scribe. "I grant you he's the best fighter in the band, the best fighter in the province, probably." He looked slyly at Little Li. "But Wu Meng isn't the chieftain, is he?"

Until now, Little Li had never wondered how the chieftain had gained control of the Tiger Mountain band. Wu Meng was, indeed, the better fighting man. But the chieftain had a natural air of command—that was it. In any crowd, he was obviously the leader, in spite of his small stature. Nevertheless . . .

"Wu Meng will become the next chieftain, and that may happen quite soon," he heard himself say.

"Why?" the scribe asked quickly. "Is the chieftain ill?"

"Well, he hasn't been himself lately," Little Li began. He

stopped abruptly. Gossiping about the chieftain, especially to someone new, was base disloyalty. Looking at the bright, inquisitive eyes of the scribe, Little Li realized that the man might not make a fighter, but he could be dangerous.

The scribe looked away. "All right, you don't have to tell me. I have to carry water again."

But before he could fetch the pails, Gao San came running up. "Little Li, the chieftain wants to see you." His lips curled in scorn. "He wants you to bring your nursling too."

Little Li and the scribe followed Gao San to one of the larger caves, where they found the chieftain, the two Wus, the butcher, and two other outlaws. The new arrivals bowed to the three officers. Little Li, feeling an undercurrent of excitement around him, guessed that another raid was being planned.

He was not wrong. "Now that all the men I want for the expedition are here, I'll tell you what we intend to do," said the chieftain. Although his face looked drawn, as if he had not slept well, his voice was crisp and confident. Little Li was glad to see the leader his usual self, once again the cunning tactician who considered every detail so that nothing could go wrong.

"We have just received word from our spy in the governor's household," said the chieftain. "The governor has ordered twenty rolls of satin from a silk merchant in the capital."

There was a stir in the cave. They all knew that a roll of silk was a very convenient form of wealth, since it packed a great deal of value into a neat, transportable form. Twenty rolls of satin, if the silk was of high quality, could feed the outlaw band for a couple of months.

The chieftain could read the thoughts of his men. "Yes, these rolls of silk are supposed to be of the highest grade," he told them. "According to our informant, the governor ordered the silk from the capital especially for his Third Lady, his newest wife."

Little Li thought he felt a movement from the scribe, who was standing next to him in the crowded cave. But when he looked at the other man's face, he could detect no change of expression. Perhaps he had only imagined the movement.

"What we will do," said the chieftain, "is intercept the silk merchant and his party three miles outside the city."

"With such valuable goods, the merchant is sure to have his own armed bodyguards with him," protested Gao San.

Most of the outlaws looked immediately at Wu Meng. They all knew the young officer would be the leader if there was a prospect of an armed clash.

"I don't expect to fight the bodyguards," said the chieftain. "We're going to take possession of the silk by a trick." He waited until he had everyone's total attention. "The merchant will be greeted by an escort of six soldiers, supposedly sent by the governor."

He pointed in turn at the six outlaws in the cave. "And you six men will be those soldiers sent by the governor."

As Little Li understood the idea, he broke into a huge smile. Several of the others chuckled.

The chieftain turned to the scribe. "You are new to our band, and normally I don't use someone untried on a raid.

But in this particular case I want you to join the expedition for the following reason. The merchant and his bodyguards will be nearing the end of a tedious journey, and they're looking forward to the amusements of the city. Most of our men here are from the countryside and know next to nothing about the city. This is where you can be useful."

The scribe grinned. He had a thin, haughty face with the pallor of someone who spent most of his time indoors. But when he smiled with genuine pleasure, his whole face came alive. "I understand my assignment," he said. "The merchant and his bodyguards must not examine the 'soldiers' too closely and remark on their countrified air. I shall be happy to occupy their attention and regale them with the promised delights of the city."

For a moment the chieftain and the scribe measured each other appreciatively. Little Li felt a twinge of jealousy. He himself had always been a favorite of the chieftain, because of his youth and his unquestioning loyalty. And now this newcomer, in the space of a day, had already gained the leader's favor.

Then Little Li grew ashamed of his ungenerous thought. The chieftain approved of the scribe because both of them preferred guile to violence. Little Li knew that the chieftain was cool and daring in action but avoided fighting whenever possible. In the four years he had commanded the outlaws of Tiger Mountain, he had achieved his successes with remarkably little bloodshed.

Now the chieftain was outlining the rest of the plan. "Once you join the merchant's party," he told the six men, "you will be watching for a chance to take the silk and run."

"We have to arrange some kind of signal so we can all act at once," said Gao San. His manner was self-important, as if he expected he would naturally be appointed leader of the party.

"Don't worry," said the chieftain. "That's all been arranged. When the right moment comes, you won't fail to know, because there will be a distraction to occupy the attention of the merchant and his guards."

Little Li was tempted to ask what the distraction would be, but the chieftain was speaking again. "The most difficult part of your task is to get away as quickly as possible with the silk, before the guards realize what has happened."

"We're not afraid of a few guards," growled one of the outlaws.

"I don't want unnecessary fighting," said the chieftain sharply. "We can't afford to lose men. These guards will be professional swordsmen, and the merchant will hire only the best."

An idea came to Little Li. "Why don't we take the silk and hide in the reeds?" he suggested. "The road to the city passes by a small lake just before the forest starts. We could quietly swim across the lake, and that way we'd have a shortcut home."

For a moment the others in the cave were too surprised to speak. Even Little Li himself was surprised. Then Gao San snorted. "Have you thought what a soaking would do to the silk? This isn't cheap cotton or hemp, you idiot!"

But Little Li had the answer to the problem. "We can inflate pigs' bladders and use them as floats. I know a pig farmer in a nearby village who has a good supply of them. The merchant is sure to have his silk well wrapped in oil cloth, and if we tow the bundles of silk across the lake on the floats, we'll manage to keep them dry."

The idea of the pigs' bladders, of course, had its source in the scribe's taunt to Gao San on his first morning in camp. Little Li looked over at the scribe, wondering if he would speak, but the scribe merely looked back at him with a faint smile and said nothing.

"Your idea is certainly worth considering," the chieftain said thoughtfully. He stroked his mustache and smiled a little, looking pleased. Finally he said, "Very well, I'm appointing you in charge of the party, Little Li."

"But he's the youngest man here!" protested Gao San angrily. "How do you expect us to take orders from a boy?"

"In this case age is less important than experience," replied the chieftain. "Little Li grew up by the Yellow River, and he can swim like a carp."

Elated by the chieftain's words, Little Li barely noticed the black looks from one or two of the others. Resentment from Gao San he expected anyway. Gao San had once been a servant of a rich family in the city, but he had been accused by his master—unjustly, he said—of stealing and had escaped to Tiger Mountain. More sophisticated than most of the younger outlaws, who were peasants, he had attracted a number of followers, the most devoted of whom was the butcher. Gao San was jealous of the growing favor shown by the chieftain to Little Li, and it must have galled him to have the young northerner named as the leader of the present expedition.

"Now then," the chieftain said to Little Li, "since you're in charge, it will be your responsibility to signal the others to seize the silk."

"May we know," asked the scribe, "what form the promised distraction will take? We shall have a better chance of preparing ourselves if we know what we can look forward to."

"No," said the chieftain. "When the distraction comes, I want you six men to be genuinely surprised—otherwise you'll arouse the suspicion of the guards. They are experienced men, and alert to tricks."

The scribe did not seem convinced, and even Little Li thought the argument weak. But before anyone else had an opportunity to object, the chieftain made a gesture of dismissal. "Little Li," he said, "your plan of swimming across the lake sounds promising. You'd better get together with the butcher and have him teach you how to prepare the pigs' bladders."

As they walked away from the chieftain's cave, Little Li looked curiously at the scribe. "Why didn't you say that inflating pigs' bladders was your idea?"

His companion waved his hand airily. "Because I was not totally convinced of the idea's feasibility. If the silk gets wet, I don't want the blame to fall on my head."

Little Li didn't know whether to be annoyed or grateful. "All right, I'll take the responsibility," he said. "And another thing: you'd better learn how to cook. I don't want to spend all my time feeding you."

In the cave occupied by the Wus, the three leaders of the band were sitting down to dinner. The chieftain had been invited to eat with Old Wu and his son, and the meal had been prepared by Old Wu's servant, a flat-faced, homely woman, but cheerful. She had prepared a creditable meal with her limited ingredients. Rice the outlaws still had, although the supply was low and she had to stretch it with millet. She had stewed some salted pork with green vegetables supplied by friendly villagers. As a special treat she served sliced duck livers, salted and sun-dried.

At the end of the meal the woman cleared away the table and left to wash the dishes. "Delicious!" said the chieftain. "Meimei is a good girl, but as a cook she needs some lessons from your woman, Old Wu."

As soon as the words left his mouth, he regretted them. He had resolved not to mention Meimei's name in Wu Meng's presence.

But the younger man showed no reaction at the girl's name. Looking steadily at the chieftain, he asked, "Why all the mystery about the distraction? I agree with the scribe, by the way, that it would be better if they knew what to expect."

"This is my plan for the distraction," said the chieftain. "The merchant's party will meet a 'traveler,' all bruised and bloody. That'll be you, Old Wu, and I know I can count on you to put on a convincing act. Whereupon Wu Meng and I will make a huge din, like the sound of a dozen men fighting."

Wu Meng nodded. "Good. That will certainly bring the guards rushing toward the source of the noise, leaving the merchant temporarily unwatched."

"You think Little Li will have the wits to recognize this as a signal to grab the silk?" asked Old Wu. "I know he's loyal, but he thinks with his fists."

"Little Li may be slow with his tongue, but he's smarter than you think," said the chieftain. "Look at his plan for getting across the lake, for instance. He's stolid, like most northerners, but he's not stupid."

"And if Little Li doesn't recognize the distraction for what it is, the scribe will," granted Wu Meng. "But why do you have to keep it a secret?"

Still ignoring the question, the chieftain asked one of his own. "What do you think caused our last raid to fail?"

Wu Meng did not hesitate. "I agree with my father's theory. We had a traitor, and the governor was warned about our intentions. That's why he had rocks substituted for the money, and that's why my father and I had the soldiers so hot on our trail."

The chieftain nodded. "Therefore our most urgent task right now is to identify the traitor. The governor has offered a huge reward for our capture, and the temptation to betray us must be pretty hard to resist."

Wu Meng looked curiously at the chieftain. "And you think you can identify the traitor while seizing twenty rolls of silk?"

"I hope so," said the chieftain. "You see, the main purpose of this expedition is not to obtain the silk, although we can certainly use it. The main purpose is to test the reliability of our spy."

"You'll have to explain," grumbled Old Wu. "And please use simple words, so even someone as senile as I am can understand."

"Listen," said the chieftain, "we're using all our best men for this expedition. The six men who are acting the part of the soldiers are the pick of our band. And then we three leaders are going to be staging the distraction. This is the opportunity the governor has been waiting for to capture all the important members of our band. He would send an army if he knew."

"I see," said Wu Meng. "And the only person who knows the whole scheme is our spy in the governor's household, the one who told us about the silk in the first place."

"Precisely," said the chieftain. "Now you know why I'm not telling anyone else that the three of us will be providing the distraction."

"But . . . but . . . " Old Wu half rose in his agitation. "This is like walking straight into the tiger's jaws!"

"Not if we're prepared for the trap," said the chieftain. "You'll act as a scout, Old Wu, to see if there are detachments of troops lying in wait for us. At the first sign of an ambush, we can still call off the raid."

"And if there are no soldiers waiting to capture us?" asked Wu Meng.

"Then that means our spy is not betraying us after all," replied the chieftain. "And the traitor is someone else, someone here in the camp."

As he walked back to his own cave, the chieftain went over the plan once more in his mind. In spite of what he had said to Old Wu, he knew the dangers were appalling. But it was desperately urgent to identify the traitor in their midst. To do that, the chieftain was willing to take risks.

4

The Narrow Escape

Little Li looked back at his ill-assorted troop. "Can't you try to look more like soldiers?"

The six outlaws were neatly dressed in brown cotton jackets with a black border, made for them by womenfolk from a nearby friendly village. But it takes more than a uniform to produce a soldierly figure, and Little Li saw that the long wait was causing the men to droop.

The raid had begun, and the men had stationed themselves on the stretch of road to the city that skirted the small lake. They could see a clump of reeds at the end of the lake where they had hidden the inflated bladders they would later use to float the silk across.

The butcher was bent over, massaging his ankles. "What's the matter with you?" Little Li asked.

"I'm not used to these boots," complained the butcher.

Little Li was also unused to the stiff leather boots. For everyday use, most of the outlaws had soft boots of cloth or skins. The stiff leather ones they now had on were army boots saved by the chieftain, the Wus, and other former regular soldiers. Little Li's own feet were hurting fiercely, for his boots, in addition to being stiff, were too small.

"Nobody else is complaining about the boots," he told the butcher curtly. "So why don't you keep quiet?"

"Listen to Little Li!" sneered Gao San. "He's only the leader of the troop for one day, and already he's acting like a chieftain. Maybe he thinks the leather boots make him look like a general!"

"Perhaps we can postpone this discussion of leather boots," suggested the scribe. "The merchant and his guards might be here at any moment."

Sullenly the outlaws resumed their watch on the road. In the afternoon sun the lake gleamed like a sheet of copper, and Little Li's chest suddenly tightened with a pang of longing for the waters of the Yellow River.

But he had no time to indulge in homesickness. His eyes, squinting in the sun, caught sight of a puff of dust in the distance. Soon some black specks appeared, which slowly grew larger and assumed the shapes of human figures and a beast of burden. The silk merchant and his escort had finally arrived.

The merchant's party were close enough to see the six men, and they were approaching warily. Little Li examined his men critically. "Don't slouch so much. And let's try to hold our spears like soldiers."

The syncopated thuds of spear butts told him the men needed considerably more practice before they would be able to pass themselves off as drilled troops.

Soon they could see the merchant leading a mule laden with cylindrical bundles—undoubtedly the rolls of silk. On

either side of him marched a bodyguard.

On seeing only two bodyguards, Little Li felt his apprehension turn to relief. This raid should be a simple affair. Was the chieftain's elaborate ruse really necessary?

But when the bodyguards came closer, Little Li changed

his mind. The two men moved with the careless grace of master swordsmen. Now they were walking ahead of the merchant, and slightly apart from each other—Little Li recognized that they were giving themselves room for swordplay. He also knew there was no way his men could overcome these two bodyguards by force. Perhaps Wu Meng might be a match for one of them, but certainly not for both of them together. Their only hope was trickery.

The two bodyguards continued to advance, their confident manner indicating alertness but not alarm. This stretch of the road was straight and totally exposed, the last place anyone would choose to stage an ambush.

When the approaching party was ten paces away, Little Li held up his hand and the outlaws behind him clumped to a ragged stop. Little Li swallowed, then walked forward and saluted the merchant and his bodyguards.

"I have orders from the governor," he said. "Word has been received that there is a great increase in the activities of bandits in this area. We are almost certain, in fact, that one of the outlaw bands has a hideout in the mountains south of here. Since you are carrying merchandise of considerable value, the governor has decided for safety's sake to send us as an additional escort for you."

Little Li was repeating the speech the chieftain had prepared for him. Although he had practiced until he knew it by heart, he had been fearful that in his nervousness he might stumble over the words. But to his surprise he found himself calm. His voice came out crisp and authoritative.

As Little Li spoke, he studied the two bodyguards. The taller one had a dark face slightly pitted by smallpox. His lips were so thin that his mouth, when closed, was all but invisible. The effect was curiously inhuman.

The other guard was younger and looked pleasanter. His roundish face was fringed with a short, bristling beard. Little Li thought him rather genial, until he saw the man's eyes. They were the coldest eyes he had ever seen.

The two bodyguards hardly changed expression when Little Li finished speaking, but the merchant broke out into a moan of dismay. "This means we might be attacked by bandits at any moment!"

"That's what you hired us for," the tall guard said calmly. "To protect you from bandits."

"Yes, but there's a whole band of them here!" said the merchant. "We might come close to their hideout!"

"Don't worry, the governor is sending us these stalwart soldiers as added protection," said the bearded guard. His tone was ironical as he passed his eyes over the six outlaws.

Little Li swallowed his resentment at the guard's sarcasm. It was true that his little troop did not inspire confidence. The butcher was standing with his mouth half open and a vacant look on his face. Even worse was the scribe, who was slouching, holding his spear gingerly as if he didn't quite know how it had appeared in his hands. But the rest of the band looked presentable enough. Gao San had a good build, and his square jaw jutted with determination. The other two outlaws, who had been in the army, gripped their spears with a professional air.

Little Li met the cold eyes of the bearded guard and managed a wry smile. "The governor has lost his best men to the wars in the north, and we have to make do with local material. But of course the outlaws have even fewer good men."

Once again he was astounded by his own fluency. Normally he had trouble getting a dozen words out. He realized what was happening: he was unconsciously imitating the speech and manners of Wu Meng, and apparently he was doing a creditable job of it.

The tall guard nodded at him. "Very well. We can use your company for the rest of the journey. My friend and I can rout a dozen bandits easily enough, but if we have a larger party, they are less likely to attempt something."

"For myself, I wouldn't mind a good skirmish," said the bearded guard. "I need some exercise."

"Oh, no, we don't want to be delayed by a fight!" exclaimed the merchant. "It's already late, and I want to reach the city before the sun sets."

The six outlaws fell in with the merchant's party, and as they walked, the taller guard and Little Li discussed the situation in the north.

"You're a northerner yourself, aren't you?" asked the taller guard.

Little Li nodded, for it was impossible to disguise his accent. "I moved south after my family was killed by the invaders," he said. There was no need to make up lies as he described the ravages of the Tartars. When he wasn't describing his personal experiences, he quoted Wu Meng.

Occasionally Little Li spared a glance at the rest of the party. The bearded guard did not condescend to address any of the outlaws. His cold, observant eyes scanned the country around him, missing nothing. If there was any sign of something unusual, he would be the first to see it.

At the rear of the party the merchant was leading his mule, and walking with him was the scribe, who was telling the merchant about the city's best restaurants and teahouses. It was obvious that the scribe spoke with an expert's knowledge.

The afternoon was far gone when they came to the end

of the lake. Little Li studiously avoided looking at the clump of reeds where the outlaws had hidden their floats. Leaving the lake behind them, they entered a dense wood. The two guards became noticeably more alert, and they kept their hands on the hilt of their swords. When the road narrowed down to a path, they walked in single file. The afternoon light, filtered through the trees, had a smoky quality. Most of the trees were conifers, pines and a few larches already turning yellow in the snappy autumn temperatures. It had not rained for several days, and the dry underbrush rustled at the slightest touch. No one concealed in the bushes could move without attracting attention.

Little Li walked immediately behind the two guards, and he thought that their reflexes and steely muscles reminded him of beasts of prey. He began to have serious misgivings about the whole scheme. Where did the chieftain plan to stage his distraction? It would have to be soon since, once past the woods, the outlaws would be in a plain where concealment was impossible. But here in the woods the bodyguards were twice as vigilant, and seizing the silk from them would be more foolhardy than plucking a whisker from the nose of a tiger.

Suddenly the tall bodyguard stopped. "What was that?" he asked.

Then Little Li heard it too: angry voices in the distance and the clash of weapons. Immediately swords appeared in the hands of the two bodyguards and they adopted a crouching stance, legs apart and ready to spring. One half of Little Li's mind admired the fluid grace of their movements; the other half wondered despairingly how the chieftain could possibly succeed in the ambush when the bodyguards were already fully alert before the attack even began.

He soon had the answer. He heard footsteps heading

toward them and cries of "Help me! Help me!"

A figure darted out from the trees, its face bloody and half covered with hair streaming from its topknot. Little Li did not recognize Old Wu until he spoke.

"Help me!" gasped Old Wu. "Our caravan is being attacked by bandits. They'll get away with all our goods!" He leaned panting against a tree and pointed behind him.

The tall bodyguard strode over to Old Wu and shook him roughly. "How many bandits?" he demanded.

Old Wu wiped at his face with his hands, smearing the blood across his cheeks. "There were at least ten men! They were hitting us with great clubs, and their leader even had a sword!"

The bearded guard bared his teeth in a smile of pure pleasure. "I think this is what we've been waiting for," he said to his companion. "Come on!"

Old Wu led the two bodyguards toward the source of the din, which seemed to be increasing in violence. As soon as they disappeared from sight, the scribe murmured, "I think this is what *we've* been waiting for."

Little Li turned to his troops. "Right. Let's get to work."

The merchant stared at the grim and purposeful faces around him and shrank back. "What . . . what . . ."

Before he could say more, Little Li hit him sharply on the jaw and the merchant slumped to the ground. The mule danced in alarm, but Gao San seized its reins and quieted it. The six outlaws quickly went to work. This was the part they had rehearsed well, and they soon had the rolls of silk unloaded and tied into six bundles.

The two bodyguards were not fools; they would soon realize they had been tricked. But by then the outlaws, and their bundles, should be safely hidden in the reeds, where the pigs' bladder floats were ready and waiting.

At this point the chieftain's carefully laid plans began to go awry. As the outlaws started to run off with the bundles of silk, the butcher turned and bent over the merchant. "I saw him carrying a fat wallet," he muttered. "Let me have a look."

"We don't have time!" urged Little Li. "Let's go!"

But the butcher was already fumbling at the merchant and thrusting a hand into the man's jacket. At his touch, the merchant stirred and opened his eyes. Suddenly he began to scream at the top of his lungs. "Help! Help! They're stealing the silk!"

Another clout from Little Li silenced him, but too late: the damage was done. The question was, how far had his voice carried? If the two bodyguards heard him and rushed back, would the outlaws have time to reach their hiding place by the lake unseen?

As Little Li bit his lip and considered, he met the eyes of the scribe, who said, "We'll have to think of a way of stopping the two bodyguards from coming after us."

The butcher was close to tears. "We can't possibly stop two expert swordsmen like that. Let's run!"

For once Gao San had no patience with his toady. "It's all your fault! Why did you stop anyway?"

There was no time to waste on recriminations. They heard running steps and the voice of one of the bodyguards. "It's a trick! I knew it! I knew it!"

As he saw the figure of the tall bodyguard appear, Little Li had an idea. "The rest of you run to the lake. I'll try to delay the bodyguards."

"You can't, Little Li!" cried one of the outlaws. "They'll make a meat patty out of you!"

"No, I have a plan," said Little Li. "If you don't run for it, we'll all be minced meat."

To Little Li's amazement, the scribe said, "I'll stay and help. The rest of you can go."

The other four outlaws didn't need further persuasion, for the taller of the two bodyguards was bearing down on them, and the bearded one could not be far behind.

"I'll be waiting over there," whispered the scribe, and sprinted for a clump of bushes.

Little Li had no time to wonder about the scribe's intentions. The taller bodyguard had seen the unconscious figure of the merchant, and as he turned to Little Li, the anger on his lipless face was demonic. Taking a deep breath, Little Li began to yell. "Bandits! There were bandits behind us too, and they made off with the silk!"

The tall bodyguard hesitated. Whether he believed Little Li or not, the momentary pause was enough. Little Li drove his spear point into the hindquarters of the mule. The animal gave an earsplitting bray and lashed out with its hoofs. The front hoof struck the bodyguard in the stomach. He doubled over, fell to the ground, and rolled in agony.

The mule bolted down the road and was just in time to crash into the bearded bodyguard, who had no room on the narrow path to move out of the way.

Without staying to see more, Little Li turned and ran. He skidded to a halt at the scribe's voice. "Here! Take the end of this!"

The scribe had unrolled a bolt of dark-colored silk and had stretched it across the road. Little Li understood the other man's plan. He crouched behind a tree on the other side of the road, across from the scribe, and took the end of the strip of silk.

He was just in time. The bearded bodyguard had disentangled himself from the maddened mule and was pounding down the road with murder in his eyes. Just as he reached the silk, the two outlaws pulled it taut. The bodyguard's reflexes were fast, but not fast enough. He tripped over the silk, somersaulted, and lay on the ground momentarily winded.

Little Li quickly stepped over to him and gave him a solid blow on the head with the butt of his spear. Meanwhile, the scribe was hastily stuffing the silk back into its wrapping. "I think we'll have time now to reach the lake."

As they ran, Little Li began to have second thoughts. "Maybe I should have run my spear through that bodyguard instead of just knocking him unconscious. If we ever meet that man again, he'll make us sorry for the trick we played on him."

The scribe frowned. "I've never killed a man, and I don't intend to start now."

"Why so righteous all of a sudden?" asked Little Li, annoyed. "You're an outlaw now, remember?" Actually, he himself had never killed anyone either, and he didn't know if he could.

For a moment the scribe did not answer, and concentrated on running. Then he turned back and looked at Little Li. "I didn't mind robbing that fat merchant. Our country is in the process of disintegration and the peasants are starving. But the merchants still think of nothing except their profits."

This Little Li knew from personal experience. When the Tartar invasion had driven him south, he had salvaged a few pieces of clothing from his gutted home and had been forced to sell them to a merchant for a small fraction of their worth. "But this merchant might make a profit anyway if he's already been paid for the silk," he pointed out. "It's the governor who'll be the loser."

"The governor is worse than the merchant!" spat the scribe. "Officials like him are so corrupt that if we cut open their bellies we'll find maggots instead of entrails."

Little Li was startled by the bitterness in the scribe's voice, and he wondered if it wasn't a private grudge against the governor that had driven the scribe into joining the outlaw band.

They said no more. When they reached the lake the setting sun sparkled over the water and dazzled their eyes. Little Li now realized that the chieftain had timed the raid so pursuers would have the low sun in their eyes and not look too closely at the reeds.

"Here!" said a voice. "We're over here!"

Guided by the voice, Little Li and the scribe groped their way through the reeds to where the other four outlaws were huddling around the floats.

"You made it!" said one of the outlaws. "How did you ever do it, Little Li?" The admiration in his voice was very flattering. Even Gao San could find nothing disparaging to say.

"It was nothing," Little Li said gruffly. "The scribe helped me."

Nevertheless, he knew that this was his first test in leadership and he had performed well.

5

The Phantom Reappears

It had not been a trap! The chieftain was nearly dizzy with relief. The governor's soldiers had not been waiting to pounce on them. The merchant and his silk were genuine, and—barring unforeseen difficulties—the outlaw band would have in its possession twenty rolls of high-quality silk. Their provisions for the winter were assured.

The chieftain's shoulders still ached from clashing swords with Wu Meng. The mock fight had to sound genuine, and the two of them had swung their weapons vigorously. Meeting Wu Meng's sword had been bone-jarring, for the younger man didn't know his own strength.

Or did he? Wu Meng kept a very tight rein on his temper, but he could have been using the occasion to vent his frustrations. The chieftain knew that the younger man fretted at being a member of a petty band of outlaws when he had once been one of the most outstanding warriors of the army. Wu Meng waited impatiently for the day when he could repay the Tartars for the humiliating defeats of the

Imperial Army. Too, there was Meimei, but here the chief-tain was less certain of the younger man's feelings. Perhaps he had only imagined Wu Meng's interest in the girl.

Massaging his aching arm, the chieftain began to make his way cautiously back to the outlaw camp. He did not wait for Wu Meng, knowing the younger man would go back separately. He might even look first to make sure that his father, Old Wu, had escaped in time from the merchant's bodyguards.

The chieftain was confident that the outlaws under Little Li would carry out their part of the plan. Old Wu might criticize him for selecting Little Li to lead the troop, but the chieftain had hopes for the young northerner. He was loyal, brave, and, in spite of his slow speech, quick to move when the occasion called for fast action. The chieftain believed that Little Li would one day make a good leader, and recently he had begun to groom him for the role.

The sun had set, and in the autumn night came quickly. If he hurried, he might arrive back at the camp before the six men with their silk. They had a much shorter distance to go, but they could not start their swim until they were certain the merchant and his bodyguards had gone. The chieftain smiled a little at the thought of the floats. It had surprised him when Little Li presented the idea. The young northerner was intelligent, but the chieftain had not thought him capable of this sort of cunning.

By the time the chieftain began the climb into the hills, it was almost totally dark. When it wasn't hidden by the trees, the quarter moon gave only a faint light, and the chieftain had to feel his way carefully. But he was driven by a sense of urgency and—he had to admit it—fear of the dark.

A tree root tripped him and he fell face down. For an instant he smelled the fragrance of crushed pine needles mixed with the rich odor of well-decomposed humus. As he sat up and brushed the dirt from his face, he heard a faint rustling behind him. Then he heard a voice, a voice that turned his warm blood into slivers of ice.

"Han Baota, my friend, why are you running away from me?" The question was followed by a giggle that sounded mad, quite mad.

The chieftain started to rise, but his legs collapsed under him. He moaned and covered his face with his hands. There was no escape. For four years he had been trying to escape his private nightmare, and now he knew it was no use.

The voice, sounding closer, echoed his thoughts. "You can't escape from me, my friend, my general. You tried to abandon me, but I'll always be standing at your back."

The chieftain raised his head. "What do you want?"

Another shrill giggle. "I want you to look at my face, at what the Tartars did to me. Come here, General Han, and take a good look."

It was almost completely dark, but the chieftain could make out a white-clad figure emerging from behind a tree. For once it looked full at him. But instead of human features, the chieftain saw only black holes on the face. He felt a shriek rising in his throat and tried to muffle it with his arm. Then he heard the giggling become softer and gradually die away in the distance. The chieftain sank down on the ground and began to shake uncontrollably.

Little Li was the last to cross the lake. As the leader and the best swimmer, he was responsible for the safety of the rest. He waited until he saw the others reach the shore on the other side before he entered the water. The men had gone over one by one, each towing a silk-laden float. On the other side the swimmers immediately clambered up the bank and ran for cover in the woods. It was better that they went separately, for they would have been more conspicuous as a group. There was a chance that the merchant or one of the bodyguards might glance in the direction of the lake, although it was more likely they would be combing the woods for the fugitives.

Crossing the lake had also given them a substantial short-cut, and the chieftain had been pleased with the suggestion. Others had looked impressed as well. As he swam in easy, powerful strokes, Little Li savored particularly the memory of Wu Meng's open approval. Additional approval would be waiting for him back at the camp when the outlaws learned how successfully he had brought off the raid, in spite of the near disaster.

Reaching the other shore of the lake, Little Li scrambled for the woods and squeezed the water from his clothes. During the swim he had been too excited to notice the cold, but now he was shivering and he tried to hurry. He had removed his boots for the swim and had placed them on top of his float. For a moment he considered not putting them back on and walking barefoot. But the ground was so prickly with pine needles that he grimaced and stuffed his feet back into the boots. Gathering his bundle of silk, he began to climb the hilly path leading to the camp.

For a while Little Li was fully occupied with his discomforts. It was hard to see the path; his clothes clung cold and wet to his skin; and, worst of all, the boots chafed his feet even more than before. He was so engrossed in his misery that he failed to notice a figure standing motionless ahead of him and narrowly avoided a collision.

It was the butcher. Little Li opened his mouth to demand what he was doing, but the butcher motioned for silence. "Do you hear it?" he asked.

Then Little Li heard it too, the sound of hoarse weeping. "Who is it?" he asked uneasily.

"I don't know," the butcher said slowly. "Maybe one of our men is hurt."

The two outlaws began to climb cautiously toward the source of the sound. They did not have far to go. They saw Gao San standing over someone seated on the ground, who was sobbing and rocking back and forth.

Little Li recognized the chieftain, and in an instant he guessed what had happened. He rushed over and put his arms protectively around the chieftain's shoulders. "Did you see it again, sir?" he whispered. "The phantom in white?"

The chieftain did not reply, but his shaking and sobbing gradually stopped. The three young outlaws looked at their leader, the butcher with embarrassment and Gao San with contempt. Little Li felt sorry the other two had seen the chieftain in this state.

Finally the chieftain looked up at Little Li and even managed a smile. "So it's you. I thought I smelled the garlic."

If anyone else had made the remark, Little Li would have been annoyed. But he only tightened his arm around the chieftain's shoulders, feeling like a mother soothing a child frightened by a nightmare. "Did you see the phantom again, sir?" he repeated.

The chieftain avoided his eyes. "I've been working too

hard lately, and my nerves are not good. I was probably startled by an owl or some small animal running for cover."

Little Li didn't believe a word of this, but he did not press the matter. He realized that the chieftain did not want to talk about the phantom in white.

The chieftain began to brush the dirt from his clothes. "Did everyone get away safely with the silk?" His voice was much steadier.

"Two of the men who swam across first must be nearly back by now," said Gao San. He looked around. "The only person I haven't seen is the scribe."

"That's strange," said Little Li. "He crossed the lake before I did."

Gao San scowled. "I don't trust that man. How do we know he won't keep the silk he was carrying and run away?"

For some reason Little Li felt an urge to defend his protégé. "You shouldn't say that without proof. I think the scribe is just slow because he's not used to the exercise."

"You are quite correct," said the scribe's voice. He stepped out of the shadows, dropped his load heavily on the ground, and leaned against a tree. "Why must our activities always be so strenuous? I'm totally exhausted! Can't we find more civilized pursuits?" For a man who claimed to be exhausted, he was not short of breath, and he would have gone on with his complaints.

But Gao San interrupted him. "Where were you? I didn't see you on the trail."

"Not being so familiar with these hills as the rest of you, I lost my way and spent some time wandering about," said the scribe carelessly. A second later he added a mighty sneeze.

The chieftain stood up. "We are wasting time! You are all in wet clothes and you will catch chills if we don't go back immediately."

For a moment Gao San did not move. He looked mutinous, as if he would have liked to pursue the questioning of the scribe. But when Little Li and the scribe both made ready to follow the chieftain, Gao San turned and fell in after them. Grumbling, the butcher followed his friend and brought up the rear.

Normally, none of the outlaws would ever think of disobeying the chieftain. Little Li found it ominous that Gao San had actually hesitated before obeying the chieftain's order. He began to fear that the chieftain's strange breakdown was costing him the respect of the men under him.

The celebration banquet was still going strong. With the silk safe in their hands, the outlaws felt free to bring out their reserves of rice and wine. The women had worked all day over their stoves, and in the evening tables had been brought out and arranged in the largest clearing. The weather was beautiful, a sunny day with just enough sharpness and movement in the air to dispel the smoke of cooking and cool the wine-flushed faces of the diners.

Toasts were given to the six successful "escort troops," who quickly responded with toasts of their own to the careful planning of their leaders. Little Li was inarticulate with pleasure, and his toast was accompanied merely by a huge grin. If I put a ball in his mouth, thought the chieftain, he would look like one of those grinning stone lions who guard temple gates. He felt a rush of affection for the young northerner.

Being childless, the chieftain wanted more than anything to adopt Little Li formally as his son, but he knew the time was not ripe for such a move. It would be interpreted by many as an announcement that he had selected Little Li as his successor. The resentment of the younger outlaws, like Gao San, was not a serious problem. It was the reaction of Wu Meng that could prove to be dangerous.

The chieftain tried to put aside such uncomfortable thoughts and share the good spirits of his men. Gao San was talking almost without stop, and the butcher echoed him whenever he could fit a word in. But however well Gao San could talk, he could not compete with the scribe.

It was the scribe who dominated the banquet. Words flowed from the young scholar—courtly, elegant phrases that dazzled the outlaws. He performed, in verse, a parody of an elaborate banquet at the home of a high official. Listening to the guffaws of the audience, the chieftain wondered if any of the outlaws heard the bitterness beneath the humor.

> *"What is life after all but a dream?*
> *And why should such a bother be made?*
> *It is better to be tipsy I deem,*
> *And doze all the day in the shade."*

The scribe raised his wine cup as he recited the poem, a quotation from the great Tang poet, Li Bai. It had also been a favorite toast when General Han and his two friends used to relax and drink together after a campaign.

The chieftain's throat tightened and his eyes automatically went to Old Wu. For a long moment the two men looked at each other. The chieftain knew that Old Wu had recognized the toast as well.

Suddenly the chieftain could no longer bear the high spirits around him. He rose from his stool, knocking over a wine cup in his haste. "I . . . I feel a little tired from the activity yesterday," he stammered, and rushed from the table.

His departure put an end to the banquet. For the moment he didn't care, although he could hear the murmurs of surprise behind him, in which Gao San's voice was the loudest.

Reaching his cave, he flung himself down on his bed and closed his eyes, trying to shut out the vision of someone in white standing in the forest, someone whose face had no recognizable features.

Sometime later—minutes, hours, it didn't matter—he felt cool fingers touching his cheek. "Are you ill, sir?" asked Meimei. "Shall I make you some tea?"

The chieftain sat up. "No, I'm not . . ." Suddenly he clutched the girl's arm. "I have to tell someone! I can't keep it to myself any longer!"

Meimei gently worked her arm free of the chieftain's tight grip. "What is it you wish to tell me, sir?"

Although he wanted desperately to talk, it was extraordinarily difficult to get the words out. "For . . . for several weeks, I've . . . I've been seeing a phantom figure in white," he said. "He says he's Zhang Ru!"

Meimei showed no surprise. "Who is Zhang Ru?"

The chieftain groaned. He closed his eyes and turned his face to the wall. After a moment Meimei rose. "I'll make some tea," she said.

When Meimei returned with the steaming cup of tea, the chieftain had made up his mind to tell her the whole story. He had no one else he could confide in. He would have liked to tell Little Li, but the northerner was too young to understand. He could not tell Wu Meng, for the younger man would only despise him. As for Old Wu, he would not be sympathetic. He had been Zhang Ru's sworn friend.

The chieftain took the cup with shaking hands, but after a few sips he became steadier. "I'll have to tell you the story from the beginning," he said.

"Old Wu, Zhang Ru, and I were friends from childhood. I was the oldest, and Zhang Ru the youngest. We were inseparable, and one day we decided to take a vow of eternal friendship. We swore we would always help one another when there was need."

The chieftain's voice faltered a little, and for a while he stared into his tea cup, remembering the past.

The three boys were in a courtyard of the Zhang mansion, where they were hiding themselves from their parents and household servants. Zhang Ru was the one who proposed the vow. He was the romantic one, and his head was full of tales from the heroic age, the Age of the Three Kingdoms.

"Remember the Peach Garden Vow of the three heroes?" he asked. His eyes were glowing. "Let's do the same thing!"

Old Wu—even then he was called that, because he liked to put on the airs of a disillusioned old man—grumbled that he had no time for childish games.

But Han Baota liked the idea of the vow. He was entering the army as an officer the following week, and he didn't know when he would see his two friends again. Old Wu was planning to enter the army later. He was a year younger than Han Baota, and his family less affluent. They needed time to gather the money necessary for equipping him and for bribing the proper officials so he could be assured of decent men under his command.

Of the three, Zhang Ru came from the wealthiest family. He was studying to take the civil examinations and would eventually follow the rest of his family into the ranks of officials.

On that quiet evening in the deserted courtyard, the three boys solemnly exchanged vows of eternal friendship. It was late autumn, and in the next courtyard the gardener was burning dry persimmon leaves. From that day on, Han Baota would always be reminded of the vow by the smell of burning persimmon leaves.

"What happened after you took the vow?" prompted Meimei when the chieftain stopped, reluctant to go on.

"We didn't see too much of one another for a while," said the chieftain. "I was too busy with the army." He smiled a little, recalling his early days as an earnest young officer, when all his efforts had been devoted to training the men under him and winning their loyalty. He had succeeded, too.

"I didn't see Zhang Ru again until I received news of his intended marriage," resumed the chieftain. "His family and mine were very close, and I took leave from the army to attend the wedding."

"What was his bride like?" asked Meimei.

The chieftain had no clear recollection of the bride's face, for she had lifted her veil only momentarily during the wedding. "All I can remember was that she was pleasant-looking," he replied, "but nothing exceptional. She was the daughter of a wealthy and influential family, and the match with Zhang Ru was very satisfactory to both families.

"I was the next to marry. My bride was the daughter of a senior army officer." He had received news two years before of his wife's death, and he remembered that the news had not affected him very deeply, for they had not been close.

"Was your wife pretty?" asked Meimei.

The chieftain looked away. It embarrassed him a little to discuss his dead wife with Meimei. "She was not bad-looking," he admitted, although he had no clear memory of her appearance. More important than her appearance was the fact that she had been barren. "My wife bore me no children, but since her father was a high-ranking officer, I was reluctant to offend him by taking a secondary wife."

"Did Zhang Ru have children?" asked Meimei.

"Yes, he did," replied the chieftain. He had made inquiries, because he had felt responsible for them. "Zhang Ru had three children. The oldest was a girl, who married some official in the provinces. There were two younger children, a boy and a girl, I believe. The boy should be about twenty, and the girl a year or so younger. I don't know what has happened to them."

It was ironical, thought the chieftain, that Zhang Ru, the one who had died, had the biggest family. He himself was childless, while Old Wu had only one son. Old Wu had been the last to marry, and from the way he spoke of his wife, it was obvious that the marriage had been an extremely happy one.

Old Wu's wife had died when their son, Wu Meng, was fifteen. By then Han Baota had risen to the rank of a general and had made Old Wu his chief captain. Lacking money and influence, Old Wu had not risen as fast as his friend. But it was different with his son. Wu Meng had entered the army upon the death of his mother, and with the help and patronage of General Han, his career had prospered— until the day of that disastrous battle.

Meimei poured more hot water over the leaves in the chieftain's tea cup, for the tea had grown cold and bitter. There was a lithe grace to her movements, and for an instant he was reminded of someone, but he could not place the resemblance. After she had poured the hot water, she returned and faced him again, her eyes curiously compelling. "You still haven't told me why you believe the phantom figure is Zhang Ru. What happened to him after you left to join the army?"

He was forced to go on. "It was in the middle of a campaign against the Tartars. I received a stunning surprise: Zhang Ru arrived and announced that he was joining the army. He was abandoning his wife and children, and a career as a provincial magistrate."

"Did he say why?" asked Meimei.

"No, but I could guess. His head was always full of romantic notions about the war." The chieftain stopped. Perhaps he had done Zhang Ru less than justice. "Actually Zhang Ru turned out to be a brilliant strategist. We were pretty happy to see him, Old Wu and I. We were reunited again, and it was like old times. The three of us worked perfectly together: Zhang Ru had his flashes of inspiration. I was the meticulous planner, and Old Wu—always grumbling—had his dogged patience. We brought off a series of successes that attracted even the attention of the emperor. Yes, things went well for a while."

"Then what happened?" asked Meimei.

The chieftain sighed. "With our successes we also attracted envy. Supplies would mysteriously fail to arrive, and always at the worst possible times. The messages we sent to the capital would get lost. Things went from bad to worse, until . . . until . . ." His voice choked on the words and he could not go on.

"Until what?" prompted Meimei.

"I . . . I can't tell you."

"What happened? What happened to Zhang Ru?"

"He's dead!" groaned the chieftain. "He's dead! Lord Heaven, I hope he is!"

"Why do you hope that?" asked Meimei. "Wasn't he your sworn friend?"

The chieftain thought of the face half seen in the darkness and shuddered. "Zhang Ru was a strikingly handsome man. If he had been mutilated by the Tartars, he would prefer to be dead!"

"Would you prefer to believe that the phantom is Zhang Ru's ghost?" asked Meimei.

"I don't know what to believe!" cried the chieftain.

"There's another possibility," Meimei said softly. "The phantom figure might be one of Zhang Ru's children coming to avenge him." She paused and looked steadily at him. "Why should he come to you?"

6

六

The Rescue of a Beautiful Girl

Little Li discovered that he was not as happy as he had expected. True, he was receiving flattering attention from the others for the part he had played in the silk expedition. Moreover, the outlaw band could look forward to a winter with adequate food and clothing. They might even be able to repay the kindness they had received from friendly neighboring villages.

And yet he was gloomy as he walked through the outlaw camp on this crisp autumn morning. He couldn't even smile when he passed the glade where the frustrated monk was trying to teach the scribe unarmed combat, a performance that normally provided entertainment for much of the camp. Today he didn't see the usual ring of spectators jeering or calling out encouragement to the scribe. Most of the outlaws were standing around in small groups, talking. Little Li had a very good idea of what they were talking about.

The chieftain's abrupt departure from the banquet the previous evening was the topic of the day. In fact, the chieftain's nervous behavior for the past few weeks was a matter of worry and increasing speculation among the outlaws.

Little Li finally decided to question Meimei. At this hour she was probably in the kitchen, a small hut with two wood stoves that the women took turns using when they cooked for large banquets or to prepare the more elaborate meals of the officers.

Normally it would be quite improper for Little Li to speak face to face with a girl who was not his close relative. But things were informal in the outlaw camp, and besides, Meimei was not the chieftain's official wife but only his mistress. Nevertheless, Little Li was usually deferential toward her because she had a natural air of refinement that kept him at a distance. Meimei had served the chieftain for only two months, but that was all the time she had needed to establish her position as the highest-ranking woman in the camp.

Since Little Li was really worried about the chieftain, however, he was determined to question Meimei. She would know better than anyone the chieftain's state of mind.

But Meimei was not in the kitchen. Little Li saw only Old Wu's serving woman, and she told hm the girl had gone to the city to visit her mother, who was sick. "What do you want to see her for anyway?" demanded the woman. "She serves the chieftain, and she doesn't have time for country boys like you!"

The avid curiosity in her eyes reduced Little Li to confusion and he retreated quickly from the kitchen.

Meimei returned that evening, but Little Li had no opportunity to speak to her. He caught a glimpse of her troubled face as she hurried to the chieftain's cave. Soon afterward the chieftain sent for the Wus, father and son. There was trouble, the whole camp felt it. The outlaws found excuses to linger in front of the chieftain's cave, where the three leaders were holding their discussion. A long time seemed to pass. Little Li dropped all pretense of doing anything useful and spent his time looking nervously at the mouth of the cave. He found that most of the other outlaws were doing the same.

Finally Wu Meng came out. He looked carefully at the men gathered in front of him; he seemed to be weighing and considering them one by one. Then he beckoned to the scribe and three of the older men who were veteran soldiers. After a moment he changed his mind and told one of the veterans to step back, while signaling Little Li to come forward. The four men followed Wu Meng into the chieftain's cave.

"We have an emergency," the chieftain told the four newcomers. "While Meimei was in the city, she heard some bad news. The governor has arrersted a serving girl in his household because he discovered she was acting as a spy for us."

Little Li was surprised. He knew they had someone in the city supplying them with information, but he had always assumed the spy was a man, a groom or a cook working for the governor.

"The name of the girl is Suying," the chieftain was saying. "She is a ladies' maid serving the governor's principal wife, and she has been working for us for more than a year."

In order to have such inside knowledge of the governor's plans, Little Li now realized, the spy had to be someone who had close contact with the governor's family. A serving girl, especially a personal maid of the family, would be ideally placed.

"She is a very intelligent girl," continued the chieftain. "She's an orphan from Fushan Village, and her uncle contracted her to the governor's mansion as a serving maid. She immediately saw possibilities in the position, and on her own initiative she offered to work for us by supplying information."

So that was who their spy was! Little Li knew that Fushan was one of the villages particularly friendly and helpful to the outlaws. A few of the villagers had even joined the Tiger Mountain band, and of the rest, most would welcome the chance to perform services for the outlaws.

"If Suying is so smart," grumbled Old Wu, "how did she get caught?"

The scribe spoke up unexpectedly. "It was our silk raid, wasn't it? Perhaps the governor had a suspicion that someone was leaking information to us. He was probably taking care that very few people knew of the arrival of the silk. Thus, when we made our raid, it may have confirmed a suspicion of his."

The chieftain looked sharply at the scribe. "Yes, that's possible," he said slowly. "The governor might even have been testing his suspicion. It's ironical that I was using the very same opportunity to test Suying's reliability."

"We must rescue the girl as quickly as possible!" said Wu Meng.

For a moment Little Li wondered if Wu Meng was fond of Suying. But the young officer's next words explained his urgency. "Under severe questioning by the governor, she might reveal all she knows about us—and she knows a great deal."

"We have a plan for rescuing the girl," the chieftain told the four newcomers. "You'll have to listen carefully, because the risks are very great."

The previous night the chieftain had seemed to be a broken man. But now, with a serious emergency on his hands, he appeared calm and resolute. His rescue plan might be full of risks, thought Little Li, but it would be carefully worked out.

The chieftain turned to the scribe. "You claim you can write in the official style. I want you to write an official document, but not just a document written by any petty official. Can you forge an imperial mandate?"

The scribe drew a sharp breath. After a moment a faint smile appeared on his face. "Yes, I think I can do it. Why, it would be something I can boast about to my children— if I live to have any children." Then he frowned. "I don't know how to forge an imperial seal, however. I shall have to see a sample, and that is not something that often falls to the lot of a lowly scribe."

"I have a sample," the chieftain said calmly.

The scribe's surprise was almost comical. Little Li was less surprised, for he knew that as a general of the Imperial Army the chieftain must have received mandates from the emperor. He woud know what an imperial seal looked like, probably better than would a provincial governor.

The chieftain got up. "Wu Meng is bringing out some old army uniforms, helmets, and armor," he said briskly. "You'll have to get busy and help him polish them. He is going to command an escort of four imperial soldiers, bearing a mandate from the court to the governor, instructing him to deliver up the prisoner Suying so she may be taken to the capital for questioning."

"I see," murmured the scribe. "Apparently the bold activities of the local bandits have aroused the interest and indignation even of the imperial court."

"Precisely," said the chieftain. "Now, you will not be one of the four men acting as escort, since you don't look anything like a soldier."

The scribe looked hurt. "I passed as one of the governor's men. Even the silk merchant's guards were deceived."

"That was different," said the chieftain. "The governor had only local men, raw recruits little better than peasants. These imperial soldiers are supposed to be elite men." He thought for a moment. "But I do want you to go separately to the city and follow the others inconspicuously. If they should run into trouble either going to or from the governor's mansion, you can show them some ways to escape. I suppose you are familiar with the streets and alleys of the city?"

"I know every passage in the city intimately," declared the scribe.

"Let's hope the city doesn't know you just as intimately," said the chieftain dryly.

Only twice in his life had Little Li visited a city. When he was still back home in the north, he had gone into the nearest town with his parents to sell some ducks they had raised. On both occasions he had been overwhelmed by its noise and color. Now he was a head taller, but he still felt dwarfed by the two-story-high city wall.

Farmers and tradesmen promptly made way for them as they entered the city gate, which was opened every day at cock's crow and closed at dusk. They made an impressive sight, Little Li knew. Each man wore a steel helmet polished as bright as silver. On their bodies they wore armor made of linked leaves of iron, with a breastplate and a backplate. Over the armor each man wore a jacket tied around the waist by a silk sash.

When taken out of storage, the armor and helmets had been badly rusted, and the jackets and sashes had suffered from moths and mildew. But Meimei and the other women had worked hard to repair the damage. Now the four men looked as trim as any soldier from the capital.

As they made their way to the governor's mansion, Little Li gazed about him wide-eyed. The city's streets were straight and crossed each other at right angles, with stores, restaurants, and stalls of every description lining both sides. Colorful cloth banners marked some of the businesses, while the more established firms had their names inscribed on wooden signs in large gilt characters. Humbler merchants stood with their wares under reed awnings or large folding umbrellas.

From all sides odors familiar and unfamiliar assailed him. A sweet burning smell drew his eyes to a candy-maker, who was spinning tiny animal shapes from melted sugar. From another direction came the pungency of pickled turnip shreds drying on reed mats. Wine shops, restaurants, teahouses, and eating booths sent out mouth-watering aromas.

Even more fascinating to Little Li were the people. Farmers came from the nearby countryside to sell their produce, which they carried in baskets hanging from balancing poles or in small handcarts. Merchants from farther away arrived with their goods on mules or pack horses. Scholars, soldiers, officials, and the idle rich thronged the streets. Unlike the peasants, who wore knee-length coats over their trousers, the well-to-do wore gowns that reached almost to their ankles.

Little Li saw very few women. Unlike peasant women, those of the upper and middle classes seldom showed their faces in public. There were a number of sedan chairs in the streets, and in his imagination the young outlaw pictured beautiful high-born ladies hidden behind the curtains. Not all the women were hidden, however. Passing a tall two-storied house decked with banners and flowers, he heard the sound of music and female voices. Several girls leaned out, their faces heavily rouged and powdered.

One of the veteran soldiers poked Little Li. "Stop staring! You look like a country boy on his first visit to town."

Little Li tore his eyes away from the pretty, flowerlike faces smiling down at him. "I *am* a country boy," he muttered.

"We're supposed to be soldiers from Hangzhou, the capital city," said the veteran. "Compared to that, this is just a backward little provincial town."

Wu Meng and the two veterans appeared splendidly indifferent to the color and clamor of the city, and Little Li tried his best to imitate them. But it was not easy. It was even harder to maintain his calm when they arrived at the gate of the governor's mansion and presented their credentials.

Was the scribe really as capable as he claimed of writing in the official style? In order to become a high official, a candidate had to pass stiff examinations in which an elegant style was essential. The scribe, by his own admission, had failed.

The scribe's forgery was apparently convincing—so convincing that the governor himself put on his official gown and received them in his audience hall. On reading the mandate, he immediately issued orders to his head jailer.

Little Li began to feel that their mission was going very smoothly. His optimism vanished when the prisoner was brought into the audience hall. On seeing the girl's condition, Wu Meng's face remained impassive, but his hands clenched for an instant, and Little Li knew he was as dismayed as the rest of them.

Suying entered the audience hall with dragging steps. As she knelt in front of the governor, Little Li looked at her back and saw the streaks of blood coming through the cloth. She had obviously been beaten. In addition, she was weighed down by a heavy wooden collar around her neck, such as those worn by criminals and enemies of the state. How could she possibly travel with them? Little Li had been prepared to carry her during the final climb into the hills, but now it seemed she could hardly walk even the level stretches.

"Take off her wooden collar," ordered Wu Meng.

So far the governor had bowed submissively to the imperial mandate and accepted Wu Meng's authority without question. But now he frowned. "This girl is a dangerous criminal, captain," he protested. "You shouldn't be deceived by her looks."

Wu Meng did not even trouble to answer the governor. "Unlock the collar," he ordered the jailer. "We have nearly a day's journey to the capital, and the wooden yoke would slow the prisoner down. I don't wish to explain to the emperor that we were delayed because we four were afraid of an unarmed girl."

The head jailer hesitated only an instant before obeying Wu Meng's command. He had not seen the imperial mandate, but his world was divided into those who gave orders and those who obeyed them. Clearly Wu Meng belonged to the class of persons who gave orders.

The governor looked disgusted, but he made no further protest. He was a well-built man in his late thirties, wearing a luxuriant beard that he stroked continually. He would part the beard in the middle, take a fistful in each hand and give each side a tug. Was he testing to see if the beard was genuine, Little Li asked himself, feeling a nervous desire to giggle.

"How did the court hear about the prisoner so soon?" asked the governor, pouting. His lips showed through the beard, and they were a deep red, almost purple. "We only arrested her the day before yesterday!"

Wu Meng raised his brows. "Surely you didn't think the central government was unaware of your troubles with the bandits? We've had our investigator in this locality for some time, and when he heard about the arrest of the spy, he immediately sent an express messenger to the capital."

The governor turned a little pale and tugged almost frantically at his beard. "The bandit problem has not been acute. Until their latest raid, I've had the situation completely under control!"

"According to our informant, your area has been infested with bandits for more than three years," Wu Meng said coldly. "Since you are not making any progress against them, the throne has decided it is time to take drastic mesaures."

Little Li held his breath. Was Wu Meng carrying his haughtiness too far? What if the governor became angry and started to look more closely at the mandate? But Wu Meng's manner became, if anything, even more arrogant. He turned to the jailer, who had removed the prisoner's yoke. "And now, if you've finished fumbling with the wooden collar, I trust we can leave? We've wasted enough time already."

The governor was now thoroughly cowed. "Can we offer you an additional escort of our soldiers, captain?" he asked, anxious to placate the imperial messenger.

Wu Meng looked at Suying, who was rising unsteadily to her feet. "I think the four of us can manage to control the prisoner," he said dryly.

The governor winced at Wu Meng's tone. Impatient to end the disagreeable interview, he turned to his guards. "Open the gate and let the imperial escort pass through!"

The girl began to stumble while they were passing the marketplace. Little Li, who was closest to her, took her arm as she seemed about to fall. "Here, let me carry you."

Wu Meng looked back and frowned. "Don't be a fool, Little Li! We can't appear to be considerate toward a prisoner. Wait until we're outside the city."

"I'll be all right," gasped Suying. "I just need to sit down for a moment."

Little Li looked around for a place where the girl could rest. He caught sight of the scribe, a short distance behind them, making urgent hand signals.

"Look, there's the scribe, sir," Little Li whispered to Wu Meng. "He seems to be pointing at the wine shop over here. Maybe he thinks this is a good place to stay."

Wu Meng nodded. He led his party toward the wine shop, a small open stall pleasantly shaded by a thatched roof. It had several square tables and wooden stools.

"Wait!" hissed one of the outlaws. "The scribe is trying to tell us something!"

The scribe was frantic. With his wild, urgent gestures, he looked like a monkey plagued by fleas. Little Li wanted to laugh, until he suddenly understood the message the scribe was trying to convey. "I think, sir, that the scribe is telling us to *avoid* that wine shop!" he whispered to Wu Meng.

But it was already too late. Two customers were sitting at a table in the wine shop, and one of them looked up at the approaching party. He had a round face fringed with a bristling beard, and when Little Li had seen him last, he had been lying unconscious on the road by the lake.

The man's eyes widened when he saw the young northerner. During their last encounter, Little Li had thought them the coldest eyes he had ever seen, but now they were burning with a fierce joy. "Well met, my fine young soldier!" shouted the silk merchant's former bodyguard, springing to his feet. "I owe you a debt, and now I can discharge it!"

His companion rose as well, and when he recognized Little Li, his lipless mouth stretched in a broad grin. "First a soldier of the governor, and now a soldier of the Imperial Army," he remarked. "Our young friend has had a quick promotion."

Wu Meng stepped forward to confront the two bodyguards. "We are on official business and have no time for distractions. If you have a score to settle with one of my men, please wait until we've discharged our errand."

At Wu Meng's arrogant tone, the two bodyguards hesitated, but only for a moment. "You've been careless in recruiting your men, captain," said the older bodyguard. "We have reason to believe this young northerner here is a robber. We'll take him to the governor for questioning."

"Not while I'm in command of these men," Wu Meng told him.

The bodyguard stared at Wu Meng. "I see," he said slowly. "You're one of them yourself! All your soldiers are . . ."

He was interrupted by the scribe's voice. "Help!" yelled the scribe. "These two men are bandits! They're trying to rescue a prisoner from the soldiers!"

"You liar!" roared the bearded bodyguard. "I've seen *you* before, too!" He whipped out his sword and lunged at the scribe.

The scribe ducked under the flashing sword, picked up a kettle of heated wine from the wine shop, and dashed it into the face of his attacker.

The bearded guard howled with pain. As he lowered his sword and put up a hand to his scalded face, Little Li struck him down with a wooden stool.

Little Li looked down at the swordsman, for the second time rendered unconscious by his hand. The debt the bearded bodyguard owed him had just been doubled, and Little Li didn't look forward to the settling of accounts. Should he kill the man now?

Little Li whirled around at the sound of clashing steel and saw Wu Meng fighting the older bodyguard. A crowd had gathered, silent and respectful; it was obvious that they were witnessing a contest between two superb swordsmen.

Wu Meng wore armor, but it hindered rather than helped him. Armor was protection against chance arrows and blows struck wildly in a battle, but not against a swordsman who knew where to find the chinks. All it did in this contest was add weight to Wu Meng's movements.

But the bodyguard also labored under a handicap: he was furiously angry, angry at having been tricked by the outlaws and robbed of the silk he had been hired to protect. His pride had been struck a serious blow, and his one aim now was to impale this bandit leader against the city gate.

The bodyguard's swordplay was dazzling, his weapon flashing like lightning. Against his opponent's furious attacks, Wu Meng looked almost motionless. When he parried, his arm moved so slightly that he did not seem to be striking aside his opponent's sword but merely causing it to slide off.

This was the first time that Little Li saw Wu Meng pitted against a really formidable opponent. What impressed him most was the beautiful economy of Wu Meng's swordplay. But at times he allowed the other man's sword to strike so close that Little Li's breath hissed and he had to shut his eyes.

Wu Meng's coolness was infuriating his opponent, and the bodyguard increased the tempo of his attacks. Then came a flurry of exchanges too fast for Little Li to follow, and suddenly Wu Meng stepped back. The bodyguard stood completely still for a moment. Then he toppled slowly to the ground, scrabbled in the dirt, and lay still.

The silence of the crowd was broken by the scribe. "Somebody should arrest these two bandits so the soldiers can go about their important business," he said officiously.

At this reminder of their duty, the guards at the city gate approached and saluted Wu Meng. "I'm sorry we left you to subdue the bandits yourself, captain. We'll take care of these two men now. You don't have to waste any more of your time."

Wu Meng nodded curtly. The four soldiers and their prisoner marched out of the city at a stately pace, resisting the temptation to break into a run until they were out of sight of the city. And as they marched it occurred to Little Li that in the fight at the wine shop the scribe had shown an unexpected dexterity quite inconsistent with the hopeless incompetence he had heretofore displayed in all the martial skills.

The scribe joined them when they reached the foothills of Tiger Mountain. Little Li had been carrying the half-conscious Suying. One of the other outlaws took the girl on his back, and Little Li stretched his arms with relief. "We didn't know you were trying to warn us away from the wine shop," he told the scribe. "We thought you wanted us to stop there."

"I know," said the scribe. "I was frantic, because I had seen the two bodyguards in there and I knew you would pass in front of the place on your way to the city gate."

"It was a good thing you threw the hot wine at the bearded bodyguard," Little Li said. "None of us was a match for him except for Wu Meng, and he was busy."

The scribe seemed anxious to change the subject. "That scrimmage would have been unnecessary if Wu Meng hadn't chosen you as one of the party," he said.

The Phantom of Tiger Mountain • 82

Little Li resented any criticism of Wu Meng. "It was just bad luck that the two bodyguards were drinking in that particular wine shop!"

The scribe merely smiled cynically, and Little Li turned away to avoid quarreling with him. In all fairness, he admitted that the scribe had been helpful in the city. Presently he found himself walking beside Wu Meng. "I was very impressed by the fight, sir," Little Li said, hoping he didn't sound impertinent. "It inspires me to work harder at my swordsmanship."

Wu Meng's face was wry. "I'm not proud of myself. I was careless in picking you as one of the party, forgetting there was a risk that you might be recognized. I only chose you because you're the strongest in the band and could carry the girl most easily."

Although Little Li now saw that the scribe's criticism was just, he was disarmed by Wu Meng's ready admission of his fault. His admiration for the young officer increased.

7

The Chieftain's Gamble

Meimei's face was grave. "Her fever is rising, sir. I'm afraid we must find a doctor for her."

The chieftain looked down at Suying, who was lying on a low cot. The girl's face was flushed and she stirred restlessly. "What can we do?" he muttered. "We don't know any doctor in the city, and even if we did, how can we keep him from informing on us afterward?"

He took the problem to the Wus, just as in the old days he would have called in Old Wu and Zhang Ru. Wu Meng was the substitute for Zhang Ru, a substitute who surpassed the original. Although he lacked Zhang Ru's more obvious brilliance, he had a harder core. He would never give way to panic.

Old Wu's serving woman prepared lunch for the three men. For the first time in many months they had chicken. It was a tough, sinewy bird, to be sure, but even so it was a rare luxury normally found only on the tables of the rich.

At the chieftain's question, the woman replied that she had obtained the chicken from a nearby village.

"How did you pay for it?" asked the chieftain, alarmed. "We've agreed not to use the silk until some time has passed, until the merchant and his bodyguards are safely away from the region."

The woman's face creased in a cunning smile. "I didn't have to pay anything. All I did was drop a hint that we've had a successful raid and expect to eat well this winter. The villagers were glad to give us the chicken as an advance."

She had simmered the chicken with bamboo shoots gathered in the wild. With cooking skills like hers, a homely face was unimportant, thought the chieftain.

"I made a rich broth with the bones of the chicken," the woman said, "and I gave it to Meimei to feed that poor sick girl."

"What do you think we should do?" he asked Old Wu. "Should we risk getting a physician from the city?"

Old Wu fingered his topknot, from which a few gray hairs were escaping. "I don't know. You're the planner here, and I just take orders."

This invariably was Old Wu's first response when asked for his advice, but he had an occasion contributed practical ideas. The chieftain waited patiently, and after Old Wu had mumbled to himself for a minute he said, "Why don't we ask the scribe to recommend a reliable physician, one who wouldn't betray us? He knows the city much better than any of us."

The chieftain looked at Wu Meng for his opinion. The younger man frowned. "I still don't trust the scribe completely. I think his pose as an effete scholar is designed to make us underestimate him."

"It's true that he took a surprisingly active part in the

silk raid," murmured the chieftain. "But if he planned to betray us, he could have done it already. Why didn't he warn the governor about the silk raid, or give away the masquerade yesterday when you were rescuing Suying? He turned out to be quite useful when you ran into the silk merchant's two bodyguards."

Wu Meng had no answer to this, although he still looked skeptical. Old Wu said, "He could be waiting for a chance to grab the whole lot of us, or at least all the important leaders."

That was possible. So far, the only opportunity for arresting the leaders had been during the silk raid—and the chieftain had made sure no one but Suying had known that he himself and the Wus were staging the mock battle that drew away the bodyguards.

"We've used the scribe twice already," said Wu Meng. "It would be unwise to rely too heavily on him."

"Perhaps you're right," admitted the chieftain. "But what shall we do about the girl? She looks very sick, and if we don't find a doctor for her soon she may die."

Old Wu's serving woman suddenly spoke up. "I know of a doctor in Fushan Village."

"A village doctor?" said Old Wu scornfully. "The villagers are all illiterate! How can one of them be a doctor?"

The woman lowered her eyes in confusion. Speaking out in front of the men had been an impertinence. Not only had she committed a blunder, but her master, Old Wu, had lost face before his chieftain.

But the chieftain was not at all offended, only interested. "Who is this physician? Does he really live in the village?"

The woman lifted her eyes, recovering some of her natural boldness. "He's a hermit called Master Feng. He doesn't live in the village, but in a small hut outside. I heard he's a very learned man and has cured many of the villagers when they were sick."

The chieftain looked at his aides. "What do you think?"

Old Wu nodded. "We may as well try him."

His son agreed. "It's less risky than looking for a doctor in the city."

Little Li accompanied Wu Meng to Fushan Village. It seemed to him that the chieftain was singling him out for more and more responsibilities lately. Naturally it was causing some resentment among the others, since he was being promoted, even if unofficially, over the heads of older men. Gao San and the butcher, in particular, were showing signs of discontent.

There were also those in the band, however, who did not grudge the favor shown to Little Li by the chieftain. A number of them had gone out of their way to praise him for the way he had conducted himself on the two recent expeditions. Surprisingly, the scribe was among Little Li's supporters. A wary friendship had developed between the young northerner and the failed scholar, a friendship interrupted occasionally by exasperation.

Little Li was exasperated because the scribe made no progress in martial arts training, despite daily practice. He suspected that the scribe had the aptitude but was too lazy to make the effort. When Little Li left the outlaw camp this morning, the scribe was lying on the ground, thrown there by his teacher, the monk. His expression seemed to say he was quite content to lie there for the rest of the morning.

So when the chieftain ordered Little Li to go off with Wu Meng, the young northerner was delighted. The mission was a welcome break from the thankless task of coaxing the scribe to work harder at his lessons. He was also glad to be doing something to help Suying. It wrenched his heart to think of the brutal beating she had received. A pleasant flutter passed through his chest as he thought of her soft cheek resting against his when he had carried her on his back. He remembered the faint perfume of her hair.

Walking down from the hills with Wu Meng, Little Li was in high spirits: he enjoyed the spongy feel of pine needles underfoot, the light falling on green furry patches of moss, the smell of a fleshy mushroom his foot had accidentally kicked. He almost bounced as he walked, and he swung his arms with delight.

In front of him Wu Meng walked quickly, lightly, with no waste of energy. Observing him, Little Li curbed his exuberance and tried to imitate the other man's easy movements. Almost as if sensing his thoughts, Wu Meng turned around and smiled briefly. There was approval in the smile, and Little Li nearly burst with pride.

Little Li was a regular visitor to Fushan Village and was on good terms with many of the villagers. While Wu Meng waited outside the village walls, he went to ask for directions to Master Feng's house. The leaders of the outlaw band rarely showed themselves to the villagers. The governor had offered a huge reward for the capture of the leaders, and while the people of Fushan were known to be friendly to the band, it was wise to minimize the risks of betrayal.

Intimidated by the city, Little Li was thoroughly at home in the village. The thatched roofs and mud walls of the houses, the fields of grain, ripe and top-heavy, the neat little vegetable plots with their rows of celery cabbages, turnips and radishes—all these were a bittersweet reminder of his own village.

There were differences, of course. In the north, his family had grown wheat in the rich soil deposited by the Yellow River, a river whose bounty sometimes overspilled and became a disastrous flood. Here in the foothills of the mountains there was no danger of flooding, but the soil was poorer. The main crop was rice, although in autumn the paddies were dry, and from a distance the yellowing rice plants looked like wheat to the homesick young outlaw.

Entering Fushan Village, Little Li walked along the dirt road that passed through the center of the village. The house he sought was larger than most of its neighbors, in size second only to the village elder's. It had three connecting rooms arranged around a courtyard, a detached kitchen, and an enclosure for animals. The whole compound was surrounded by a fence.

This was the residence of the Pig Woman, so named because she was a widow who had made a success of raising pigs. She was so successful that a go-between had just concluded negotiations for a match between the Pig Woman's only son and a lovely girl from the next village.

The Pig Woman welcomed Little Li with a wide grin that showed all four of her remaining teeth. No two of the teeth met when she closed her jaws, but that didn't prevent her from heartily enjoying her own pork. Little Li called often at her house because she had planted a small patch of ground with garlic and kept him supplied. Since he was the same age as the Pig Woman's son, he interpreted her warmth toward him as purely maternal in nature.

"Look at these!" cried the Pig Woman, thrusting two garlic bulbs at him. "I've been drying them for you. Each clove is as large as a pigeon's egg!"

Little Li gladly accepted the garlic bulbs and, after thanking her, asked for directions to Master Feng's house.

The Pig Woman looked anxiously at him and ran her hands over his chest. "Master Feng's house? You're not sick or hurt, are you?"

Little Li backed away. When she patted him over like that, he felt like one of her hogs. He was relieved when her son, the Pig Boy, entered the house. Seizing the opportunity, he congratulated the boy on his coming marriage and asked him the way to Master Feng's house. With the directions and with the precious garlic bulbs, the young outlaw escaped before the Pig Woman could press him to stay.

Little Li joined Wu Meng at the edge of the village, and the two men walked a short distance to a thatched cottage of yellow clay situated by a stream. The door was open, but the cottage was empty. Looking toward the stream, they found Master Feng by the bank, fishing. The hermit wore a large basket hat, and as he sat hunched over, all they could see was his long white beard.

Wu Meng approached and cleared his throat. "Please

excuse our intrusion, Master Feng. We are in urgent need of your help."

Without looking at the two outlaws, Master Feng said, "You're disturbing the fish."

His line jerked slightly, and Little Li was astonished to see that there was no hook or bait at the end of the line. "How do you expect to catch fish if you don't use any bait?" he couldn't help asking.

"What makes you think I'm trying to catch fish?" retorted the hermit.

Little Li had heard that learned men like Master Feng were often eccentric—the more learned, the more eccentric they were. He decided to keep quiet.

Wu Meng spoke again, his voice still soft and courteous. "We have a young girl who is sick and needs medical attention."

The hermit finally looked up at them. He had long white droopy eyebrows, and through them his bright eyes sparkled like little bits of mica. "You're not from the village," he said. "I help only the villagers."

"The girl may die," said Wu Meng.

Master Feng dipped his baitless line in the water again. "What of it? It may be better for her to die than to continue living in this wretched world."

Outraged, Little Li opened his mouth to protest, but Wu Meng spoke first. "I'm sorry to have wasted so much of your time, Master Feng. Please forgive our rudeness." He maintained his quiet, even tone throughout.

Little Li waited for Wu Meng to make another appeal to Master Feng's humanity, but to his astonishment the young officer turned and began to walk off. After a moment Little Li followed him.

Master Feng's voice stopped them. "Wait! I'll come with you."

As the two outlaws led Master Feng to their hideout, Little Li reflected that he had learned another lesson from Wu Meng. If he had lost his temper and shouted at Master Feng, the hermit would have refused to help them. Perhaps the hermit had been deliberately testing the temper of his visitors.

Little Li worried about what Master Feng's reaction would be when he learned that they were outlaws. Would he turn back and go home? He need not have worried. When they reached the secret pass, Master Feng showed no surprise at all when Wu Meng and the lookout exchanged signals. Nor did he change expression when the three men arrived at the caves. Little Li realized that Master Feng had already guessed what they were, probably as soon as he had set eyes on them.

When the chieftain heard the arrival of Master Feng, he left his cave and went in person to welcome the hermit. He had met eccentrics of this sort before and knew they were often quite testy. It was best to treat them with all possible courtesy. Many of them had been men of learning and rank in former life and still expected deference wherever they went.

The chieftain clasped his hands and bowed deeply to Master Feng. "Please forgive us for disturbing you, Master, and asking you to come into these uncivilized hills. May we offer you some tea to refresh yourself after your steep climb?" Unconsciously he had spoken in the formal language he had once been accustomed to use with officials.

Master Feng waved away ceremony. "The climb didn't bother me; I'm used to exercise. Let me see the patient."

The chieftain had met learned physicians who discoursed at length on the philosophical nature of the illness, but whose only contact with the patient was to feel the sick man's various pulses. He was glad Master Feng omitted the lecture and used a more direct approach. As a soldier, the chieftain knew that the wounded needed not philosophy but prompt treatment.

Master Feng took only the pulse at Suying's wrist. Then he gently turned the girl over and uncovered her back. It was an ugly sight: the welts were inflamed, and some of them were covered with dark scabs. Master Feng pressed at a scab and some grayish pus oozed out. Suying moaned but did not open her eyes.

"What do you think, Master?" the chieftain asked anxiously.

Master Feng rubbed his forehead. He had removed his hat on entering the cave, and had uncovered a lofty forehead, distinguished by two huge bumps. Finally he sighed. "I need some medicine to draw out the poison. My supply is all used up."

"We'll buy some," the chieftain said immediately.

"It's extremely expensive," the hermit said, and peered at the chieftain with his small bright eyes. "And you have to buy it from an apothecary in the city."

That was awkward. At the moment it would be hazardous for members of the outlaw band to venture into the city.

Furthermore, they had almost no ready cash left, their sole resources being the rolls of silk.

"Would you please excuse me, Master Feng?" said the chieftain. "I must talk to my associates."

Old Wu, when the chieftain consulted him, agreed that buying the medicine was difficult. The outlaws had heard that after Suying's rescue the governor had imposed much tighter security on the city. Any stranger venturing into its gates would be closely examined.

"Perhaps we can ask one of the villagers to go," suggested Wu Meng. "The son of the Pig Woman regularly sells pork in the city. We could ask him to buy the medicine for us, under the pretext of bringing meat to the market."

The chieftain nodded. "That might work. But how can we pay for the medicine? Master Feng says it's very expensive, and we have almost no cash left."

The eyes of all three men went to the corner of the cave where the rolls of silk were neatly stacked. "It's too soon to use the silk," said Wu Meng. "The silk merchant and his bodyguards may still be in the city. What if they should see the silk and recognize it?"

"But we don't have any choice!" protested the chieftain.

"The risk is too great," said Wu Meng. "We can't let the safety of our whole band be jeopardized for the sake of one girl."

"If the life of one member means little to you, how can you care about the rest of the band?" asked the chieftain.

"It's not merely the welfare of this little band of outlaws," said Wu Meng. "This band may someday be the instrument to help free our country of invaders! We have to think of the welfare of our nation!"

Not for the first time did the chieftain feel there was

something inhuman about Wu Meng. Although the young officer was a magnetic leader and a superb fighter, he lacked an essential element: compassion. He would lead his men to glory, but he wouldn't notice whether they were hungry or hurt, or whether their feet were wet.

"The girl Suying risked her life to work for us," said the chieftain. "I'm willing to use the silk for purchasing the medicine."

The argument continued, and after a while the chieftain turned to Old Wu. "What do you think? Is it too risky?"

Old Wu pulled at his mustache and refused to meet the chieftain's eye. "I'm afraid I agree with my son." After a moment he added, "If Zhang Ru had been here he would have agreed with you. He generally took your side."

The remark cut deeply. Of course Old Wu had not meant to hurt him by mentioning Zhang Ru, but for an instant the chieftain saw again the figure in white and heard the high-pitched giggle. Making an effort to recover himself, he again argued for using the silk to purchase the medicine.

The voices of the three leaders were clearly audible outside the cave entrance. Little Li found reasons to linger near the cave, and he was not the only one to overhear the heated discussion.

"The chieftain is too rash!" muttered Gao San. "He could get us all into trouble!"

"That's not true!" said Little Li. "He's thinking only of our welfare!"

The northerner found himself torn. He respected the chieftain as a second father, but on the other hand his admiration for Wu Meng approached worship. He was deeply distressed to find Wu Meng ready to sacrifice the girl. He looked at the scribe, wanting to know what the other man thought of the dispute.

The scribe's face looked unusually stern and determined, almost as if he had come to an important decision. Little Li touched him on the shoulder. "Who do you think is right? The chieftain or Wu Meng?"

With a start, the scribe came to himself and looked at Little Li. "Who is right? It depends on what you think is important." For once the scribe was completely serious, and he spoke without any of his usual flowery phrases.

Little Li was about to ask him what he meant when he caught a murmur of voices behind him. He turned and saw that Gao San, the butcher, and half a dozen other men were huddled in earnest conversation.

"The council of monkeys is in session," murmured the scribe, returning to his usual manner. "We should be alert for trouble."

Little Li laughed. The group of outlaws, squatting on their haunches with their knuckles resting on the ground, did indeed look like monkeys.

At the sound of Little Li's laughter Gao San turned, and something about the expression on his face made Little Li uneasy. He got up and walked over to the circle of men, who looked to him very like conspirators. "What are you up to?" he demanded.

Gao San glowered but kept a stubborn silence. The butcher was less restrained. "We're talking about replacing the chieftain. He's showing signs of losing his mind."

Little Li was shocked. He knew that everyone in the band had noticed their leader's nervous attacks, but he hadn't realized the extent of the disaffection with the chieftain. "The chieftain is simply on edge," he said. "You can't blame him for that. He's certainly got enough to worry about."

"Just a little on edge, is he?" sneered Gao San. "Then what do you call his behavior on the night we raided the silk merchant? The chieftain was rolling on the ground crying hysterically. You saw him yourself!"

Little Li was desperate to explain that the chieftain's condition was the result of encounters with a phantom, but he remembered that the chieftain himself was reluctant to discuss the subject. Was it associated with something shameful in his past? Something that would make the others despise him even more? Finally Little Li said, "You won't be able to replace the chieftain. There's nobody else here as good as he is."

"There's Wu Meng," Gao San said, and several voices murmured agreement. "We need a younger, more active man anyway."

"Wu Meng is a great warrior, but that doesn't mean he would make a good chieftain," said Little Li, deeply disturbed at having to choose between the two men he admired most in the world.

"You just side with the chieftain because he favors you!" jeered the butcher. "You're his pet dog, always ready to trot over at his call!"

Little Li ignored the taunt. "The chieftain was a great general," he said. "We need a man like that for our leader."

"He used to be a great general," retorted Gao San. "But now's he just an old man who's losing his wits."

"I beg to disagree," drawled the scribe, coming over to join the group. "The man who planned the silk raid and the rescue of Suying is not a dotard losing his wits."

"Your opinion doesn't count!" snapped Gao San. "You're

just a fop from the city, and you can't even wrestle a scared rabbit! Only a fighter counts around here!"

"In that case you'd better count me," said a deep, hoarse voice. The circle parted to admit the monk, his bare head and neck still glistening with sweat from hard exercising. "What's this about choosing a new chieftain?"

"Gao San and some of the others want to depose the chieftain and make Wu Meng our leader," Little Li told him.

The monk wiped his neck with a kerchief. "Well now . . . do we have any particular reason for the change?"

Several people started to speak at once. The monk motioned for silence and pointed at Gao San. "All right, what's your complaint about the chieftain?"

"He's been acting strangely," Gao San said sullenly. "We don't trust his judgment anymore."

"Acting strangely?" said the monk. "We all act strangely sometimes. That Master Feng who came today acts strangely. The scribe here acts strangely—I know he can master kung fu, but he just refuses to learn. *I'm* acting strangely right now by listening to your foolishness!" With that he stalked off.

The men in the circle looked at one another somewhat sheepishly. "Come on, let's go," urged Little Li. "We've got work to do."

As the men began to disperse, the chieftain came out of the cave. Beckoning to one of the outlaws he said, "Go to Fushan Village and fetch the Pig Boy. I need him for an errand to the city."

Behind the chieftain stood Wu Meng, looking grim. Old Wu's face held no expression at all.

8

A Threat to a Village Ally

The Pig Boy was indignant when he handed over the medicine to Little Li. "The apothecary charged me five times the proper price!" he said, sputtering.

The young outlaw was resigned. "It couldn't be helped. We were in no position to bargain." Only a handful of silver was left after the transaction, and Little Li gave the village boy a third of it. "That's for your trouble, and for the risks you took."

As the Pig Boy bowed and protested at the generous reward, Little Li had another thought. "Did the apothecary look surprised at all when you showed him the silk?"

"He certainly did!" replied the Pig Boy. "He unrolled the whole length to make sure it wasn't cotton cloth with only a bit of silk at the outside end. I was insulted!"

Little Li couldn't blame the apothecary for being suspicious. It was highly unusual for a bolt of such high-quality silk to fall into the hands of a pig farmer, even a prosperous one. There was bound to be talk. The purchase of the medicine was a risky move, just as Wu Meng had said. Well, what was done was done, and Little Li refused to have regrets. They had a responsibility toward the sick girl.

The Pig Woman was still outside feeding her pigs, and the young outlaw took the opportunity to leave quickly, before she could come back in. He wanted to avoid her overwhelming hospitality—at least until his supply of garlic ran out.

The medicine, however costly, was effective. The day after he started administering it, Master Feng emerged from the cave where the patient lay, clapped his hat on his head, and announced that he was ready to go home. The girl was out of danger. Little Li was summoned to escort him back.

"Please stay awhile and rest, Master," begged the chieftain. "You must be tired after your long vigil."

The hermit refused to linger. "I'm not in the least tired, and besides, I want to go back to my stream. The fish are waiting for me."

Nor would he accept any payment for his services. "You'll have another debt to discharge soon enough," he told the chieftain as he was leaving.

Little Li puzzled over the remark almost all the way back to the village. Being somewhat in awe of Maser Feng, however, he was at first afraid to ask for an explanation. Finally, when they were nearing the hermit's hut, curiosity overcame him. "What is the debt we'll soon have to discharge, Master?"

The hermit did not reply immediately. He entered his hut, took down his fishing pole, and went to the stream. Only when he was comfortably seated on the bank and his line was dipped into the water again did he look up at Little

Li. "Your debt is to the villagers of Fushan, for the danger you brought upon them. Now go away and don't bother the fish."

Suying recovered so quickly that after two days she was able to leave her bed. The first thing she did on getting back on her feet was to seek out her rescuers and thank them for saving her.

Little Li was teaching the scribe how to cook when the girl approached. The scribe was fanning the flames of a small wood stove set on the ground outside their cave. An iron pan rested on top of the stove, into which Little Li poured a small amount of oil. The fire was now going briskly, and the scribe picked up a dish of cut vegetables. Cutting vegetables was one task at which he proved surprisingly skillful. Little Li's only complaint was that the scribe spent too much time trying to make the shapes of the pieces symmetrical.

"The oil is hot enough now," said Little Li. "Put in the vegetables."

The scribe dumped the vegetables into the smoking oil with a splash, and a fountain of oil droplets rose, spattering them both. "You didn't have to throw in the vegetables so hard!" yelled Little Li. His hands and face stung with dozens of tiny burns.

Sullenly, the scribe wiped the oil from his face. "You neglected to tell me I had to introduce the vegetables into the oil gently."

Little Li stirred the sizzling vegetables furiously. "Any fool would have known without being told!"

At the sound of a girl's laughter they whirled around.

Suying controlled her face and bowed deeply. "Please excuse me for disturbing you. I've come to thank you both for rescuing me from the governor's prison."

Little Li's heart made a neat somersault. Then he jumped up and rushed to the cave for a stool. "Here, you'd better sit down!" he said, guiding the girl gently to the stool. "You're still weak."

Suying sat down gracefully and smiled. Her smile was enchanting. Little Li's legs felt like jelly, and he began to think he needed the stool more than she did. But before he could move, he caught a strong smell of burning. He turned quickly to the stove, but it was too late. A column of oily black smoke rose from the iron pan. He had just enough presence of mind to wrap a piece of cloth around his hand before grabbing the pan from the fire and turning it upside down on the ground.

When the smoking finally died down, Suying said in a small voice, "It's all my fault for coming just now. Can I help you in any way?"

The scribe peeked under the pan and sighed. "Yes, you can help me cut more vegetables."

"She's too sick to work!" protested Little Li. He turned to Suying. "Please rest on the stool. We'll soon clean up this mess."

Suying watched in amusement while Little Li scrubbed the scorched pan and the scribe prepared more vegetables. She was as pretty as Meimei, Little Li decided, but in a different way. Her mouth was slightly larger and her features were more strongly marked. The greatest difference was in demeanor. Whereas Meimei was always composed and serious, Suying seemed to sparkle with humor. When he had carried her on his back, Little Li had noticed that her muscles were well toned. It probably meant that though she was slightly built, she had had some training in combat. He already knew of her courage.

Little Li was piqued to see that Suying's attention seemed to be more on the scribe than on himself. Watching the scribe washing vegetables, she said, "You can't be a country boy—your hands are too fine. And you certainly don't talk like a peasant. Are you from the city?"

"Yes," said the scribe. He didn't look up from his scrubbing.

"Why did you join the outlaw band of Tiger Mountain?" asked Suying. There was curiosity in her eager glance and also—to Little Li's chagrin—unmistakable admiration.

"I joined because I thought it would be a romantic adventure," said the scribe curtly. Usually, when questioned about his reasons, he would spin elaborate tales, each one more improbable than the last, to explain why it had become necessary for him to leave the city. But for some reason he was ill at ease with Suying. This was the first time Little Li had seen him ill at ease with anyone.

On thinking it over, the young northerner thought he knew why. The scribe belonged to a social class where women were divided into two groups, serving women and equals. The serving women he could treat with familiarity, but those who were his equals—except for immediate relatives—he saw only from a distance. Suying was speaking freely to him but on equal terms, and that made her hard to classify. For a serving girl she was too pert, and for a social equal she was too direct. No wonder the scribe was at a loss.

Little Li was sorry for the girl, since he could see that she was hurt by the scribe's apparent coldness. He began to ask her about her life in the governor's household. "How did you happen to work for the governor in the first place?" he asked. "Wasn't it hard for a country girl to enter the inner chambers of an official?"

"It wasn't easy," Suying admitted. "Wealthy city families often hire peasant girls for kitchen work or cleaning duties. Last year, when the governor's men were looking for girls in our village, I offered to go. Your chieftain had already mentioned that it would be a good idea if the outlaw band could put someone in the governor's kitchens for general information about the city."

"But you did much better than that," said Little Li.

Suying nodded happily. "I was lucky. The governor's First Lady wanted a new hairdresser because her old one was clumsy and always pulled her hair when she combed out the snags. I happened to be sweeping the courtyard when I heard her complain, so I spoke up and said I was a good hairdresser."

"The First Lady must have been surprised," remarked the scribe. "Cleaning women don't often speak up without being addressed first."

Suying didn't look in the least abashed. "Yes, she was pretty surprised, but she didn't scare me."

"I'm sure she didn't," murmured the scribe.

"Well, I'm quite good at combing hair," Suying said cheerfully. "I used to do my mother's hair, and since she often had headaches, I massaged her scalp and neck. She loved it. When I tried it with the First Lady, she loved it too. That's how I became her regular hairdresser."

"Was it hard to gather information about the governor's plans?" asked Little Li.

Suying grinned. Her eyes sparkled, and the corners crinkled in a way that reminded Little Li of a mischievous child. "It was quite easy for me to get inside information. You see, the First Lady is four years older than the governor—it was one of those childhood marriages—and he's a little afraid of her. He tells her all his plans, and then she tells me. She enjoys my combing and massaging so much that she can sit in front of the mirror and talk to me for half the morning."

"When we made the raid on the money box, the governor substituted rocks for the money, didn't he?" asked Little Li. "You didn't warn us in time, and the chieftain was very upset about that."

Suying looked puzzled. "I didn't hear about the rocks. I thought you pulled off the raid quite successfully."

"What?" exclaimed Little Li. "When we opened the box we found it full of rocks!"

"But . . . but . . ." stammered Suying, "the governor lost the money! He was furious!"

Little Li was dumfounded, and the more he thought about Suying's revelation, the less he liked its implications. He knew that the chieftain had at one time suspected Suying of betraying them and collaborating with the governor to use the money box as a decoy. That theory had proved false and the chieftain should be told immediately. But then, what did happen to the money?

"Maybe you didn't know all about the governor's plans," he suggested. "Or maybe he didn't tell his wife everything."

Suying frowned. "I suppose that's possible. Ever since his

Third Lady entered the household, the governor has been seeing less and less of his first two wives."

"What's the Third Lady like?" asked the scribe. There was something a little strange in his voice.

"She's lovely," said Suying. "The governor is quite infatuated with her."

"We know," said Little Li. "He ordered twenty rolls of expensive silk for her."

Suying grimaced. "It was the silk that got me into trouble. The governor wanted the gift to be a surprise, and he told no one except his First Lady. She told no one except me. So when you seized the silk, they were able to trace the leak to me."

"I'm sorry about what happened," said Little Li lamely. He was unable to express adequately the horror he had felt when he had seen her dragged into the governor's audience hall, all bloody from her beating.

"You got me safely away," Suying said lightly. "And with all that silk, you don't have to worry about the coming winter."

"Imagine," said Little Li slowly, "the money the governor spent on his Third Lady will feed our band for months! I suppose she's pretty vain. Any woman would be, to have the governor under her control like that."

Suying looked thoughtful. "Actually, she isn't vain at all. I've always found her gentle and quiet, and a little sad. I don't think she is very happy, in spite of the governor's attentions."

There was a clatter. The scribe had dropped the knife he was using to cut radishes and was sucking his finger.

"You've cut your finger!" cried Suying, all concern. "Let

me see. I can bind it up for you . . ." Her voice trailed to a stop, and she stared.

Little Li stared too. He saw that the scribe looked different somehow. It was as if all these past weeks he had been wearing a mask and now the mask was dropped, leaving his face naked and exposed.

"You knew her, didn't you?" exclaimed Suying. "You're acquainted with the Third Lady!" Then her eyes widened. "Were you lovers?"

The scribe had torn off a scrap of cloth from his neck scarf and was tying it around his bleeding finger. "She is my sister," he said softly, without looking up.

Little Li had many theories about the scribe's background, but he had never thought of this. "Then how . . . why did you join our Tiger Mountain band? Since your sister is the governor's favorite, your whole family should benefit! Your father's position is sure to rise!"

"My father is dead," the scribe said shortly. "As for my family, I had been hoping to retrieve our fortunes by passing the official examinations. I hadn't expected it would be through my sister's selling herself to the governor."

Little Li recalled that the scribe had said he failed the examinations because he had written some bawdy verses in the examination papers. At the time he had thought the scribe was being facetious. Now he realized it could be the truth. Perhaps, hearing of his sister's marriage to the governor, he had written the verses in bitterness and disgust, and had deliberately failed the examinations.

"Does your sister know you've become an outlaw?" he asked.

"No, she thinks I've gone north to join the army," said

the scribe. "She probably thinks I'm fighting the Tartars at the moment." For an instant his face tightened with anguish and Little Li, unable to look on it, turned away.

"I hope the governor never learns what you've done," said Suying with feeling. "He may be infatuated with your sister, but if he finds out you are a member of this outlaw band, things may go hard with her. This band has been the chief source of trouble in his district."

Little Li was sure that the scribe had suffered over this point already and needed no reminder. He quickly picked up the dish of cut vegetables and put the iron pan back on the grill. "Come on, let's get on with our cooking lesson. Otherwise we'll still be on our noon meal while everyone else is starting tomorrow's breakfast."

The scribe added a few more twigs to the fire and fanned it back to life. Little Li added more oil to the iron pan. "Now put in the vegetables," he told his pupil, "but gently, so the oil won't spatter."

With generous advice from both Little Li and Suying— sometimes contradicting each other—the scribe began to stir-fry the vegetables. "Look out!" he hissed at Little Li. "You're jogging my elbow!"

A sudden idea struck Little Li. He went to his niche in the cave and came back with a handful of chopped garlic. "Here, this will add some flavor." A pungent odor rose from the pan as the garlic sizzled in the hot oil.

"That's barbarous!" cried Suying. "Adding garlic to stir-fried vegetables!"

Little Li was hurt. "This is the way we always did it at home."

"Yes, but this is not the north," retorted Suying.

In the matter of garlic the scribe sided with Suying. The three of them were still arguing when they smelled burning, and again they saw a column of black, oily smoke rise from the iron pan.

Before they could finish scrubbing the pan for the second time, they heard the voice of Gao San, announcing disastrous news. "We just got word from Master Feng! The governor's soldiers have occupied Fushan Village, and they're threatening to execute all the inhabitants!"

9

九

The Chieftain's Guilty Secret

Since Gao San's voice had carried all over the camp, it was not possible to keep the news a secret. The chieftain decided to call a general meeting of the whole band to discuss the emergency.

As he watched the outlaws gathering in the clearing, the chieftain felt like an old man of seventy years, although he was barely fifty. He should have retired and given way to a younger man like Wu Meng. Age had dulled his mind and caused the present disaster. Wu Meng had warned him, but he had not heeded the warning.

But when the outlaws were all assembled, the chieftain straightened his back. He would retire, but not before he had brought them out of the present calamity. Since he had caused it, it was his responsibility to overcome it.

The messenger from Master Feng was brought forward to give his report. He was a villager, sent by the hermit as soon as he had seen the soldiers marching toward Fushan Village. Master Feng had anticipated the governor's move.

Which was more than I had, thought the chieftain. He had sharper wits than I, and he's even older. It was not old age in my case: it was sheer stupidity.

"What was the reason given by the soldiers for their action?" the chieftain asked the messenger.

"The officer said he had proof our village was collaborating with the outlaws," said the messenger. He was staring around with wide eyes. This was the first time he had been to the hideout of the famous Tiger Mountain band.

"And what was the proof?" asked the chieftain, although he had a premonition of the answer.

"It was the roll of silk," said the messenger, just as the chieftain had feared. "An apothecary in the city received the silk as payment for some medicine, and he mentioned the fact to his friends. Talk started and reached the ears of a silk merchant from the capital."

There was a murmur among the outlaws. Almost all of them had heard the discussion between the chieftain and Wu Meng over the risks in using the silk.

The chieftain forced his expression to remain impassive. "And then?" he prompted the messenger.

"The merchant rushed over to look at the silk, and he recognized it as his own ware that was stolen from him," finished the messenger.

A groan came from someone in the crowd, but more disturbing were the gloating looks from several others. The chieftain forced himself to meet the eyes of Wu Meng. The younger man looked grave, but there was no triumph in his face, although he had been proved right and his chieftain wrong.

"So the governor must have traced the silk to the Pig

Woman's son," murmured Wu Meng. "Why didn't he arrest the boy? Why threaten a general massacre?"

The messenger drew a shuddering breath. His family was among the villagers, and the doom hanging over them must be weighing heavily on him. "The soldiers did not say, but Master Feng's theory is this: there are close ties between our village and your band, and some of your members are originally from Fushan. When the news reaches you, those outlaws might want to desert you and offer to help the soldiers attack this stronghold in return for mercy toward Fushan Village."

A deep silence fell over the clearing. That's exactly what I would expect if I were in the governor's place, thought the chieftain. It required an effort to speak, but he had to know. "How much time will the villagers have before the executions start?" he asked.

"Three days," the messenger said huskily. Without warning, he burst into tears.

All over the camp the chieftain could hear whispers, and he could guess what the whispering was about. His men were all discussing the threat hanging over Fushan Village, and the possibility of desertions. In one brilliant move the governor had created fear and distrust within the ranks of the outlaws. It was the worst crisis ever faced by the Tiger Mountain band, and it did not help the chieftain's state of mind to know the blame was his alone.

He could hear the deep voice of Wu Meng talking to some of the men, cheering them, bracing them, trying to restore their morale. The young officer's behavior toward the chieftain had been impeccable. Not by a glance or a word had he hinted that the crisis would not have arisen if his advice had been followed.

For a moment the chieftain considered surrendering himself to the governor in exchange for lifting the sentence on Fushan Village. He knew, however, that the governor would not be satisfied with his surrender alone, but would require him to hand over Old Wu, Wu Meng, Little Li, and other leaders of the band. That the chieftain could not do. He could never betray the men serving under him.

He could not share his trouble with anyone. Normally he would have called in the Wus, but they were the ones who had argued against using the silk to buy the medicine. He would not be able to bear it if they reproached him, and he could bear it even less if they studiously avoided reproaching him.

If only Little Li had been a few years older! The chieftain felt a growing affection for the young northerner who took the place of the son he never had. Little Li was sympathetic to his feelings and aims, more so than Wu Meng. But he was much too young to share the burden of the present crisis.

Sometimes at night the chieftain talked freely to Meimei. Her quiet, self-contained, uncritical presence soothed him. How would she view the problem of Fushan Village? She was from the city, but she was on close terms with Old Wu's maid and other women from the village.

That evening she served his dinner with her usual deft efficiency. He could read nothing in her tranquil face, a face more delicately formed than those of the other women in the camp. From the time she had entered his service, she had behaved as if her sole function was to look after his comfort. But tonight she had no comfort to give.

The chieftain had little appetite for the meal. When Meimei cleared away the dishes, he rose abruptly and left the cave. He had to get away from the whispers in the camp. Aimlessly, he plunged into the hills, conscious only of the need for violent exercise, for distraction from the gnawing guilt inside him.

Some time later he found himself standing in front of the waterfall. From the weakness and trembling of his legs he knew he had walked a long way, and from the thick darkness around him he knew that the evening was far advanced. He had come to the waterfall, but not by accident. There was someone he expected to see.

He sat down on a rock, grimacing at the twinge in his arthritic knee. It was colder now than it had been when he last had come here. Winter was nearer. The fine spray from the waterfall stung his face like tiny needles, and soon the chill penetrated his clothes, his skin, and even his flesh, reaching to his very bones.

He peered intently at the waterfall, trying to see a white figure beyond it. "Zhang Ru, are you there?" he whispered.

The soft, high laughter sounded behind him. "Of course I'm here. You're expecting me, aren't you?"

The chieftain turned and saw the white figure, not behind the waterfall this time, but standing beside a larch tree. Branches of the tree covered the face, so that the chieftain could not make out its features. It was too dark in any case for a clear view.

"How does it feel," said the soft, mocking voice, "to have

The Chieftain's Guilty Secret • 115

the death of a whole village on your conscience? You left me to the mercy of the Tartars. Now will you leave the village of Fushan to the mercy of the governor?"

"What should I do?" the chieftain asked dully.

"What should you do? Why not repeat what you did before? You deserted the army four years ago, and now you can desert the outlaw band. They are better off under a different leader, wouldn't you say?"

The chieftain moaned and covered his face with his hands.

Little Li left the meeting with his mind in turmoil. The news about the occupation of Fushan Village had strengthened the hand of those arguing for the removal of the chieftain as leader of the outlaw band. Wu Meng's judgment had been proved right. Little Li remembered the suffering on the face of the chieftain when he heard the messenger, and his own heart ached with sympathy. He still could not blame the chieftain. The alternative had been to leave Suying without medical help, and to Little Li that was unthinkable, especially now that he had grown to know the girl and to admire her spirit.

But Little Li also ached for the villagers of Fushan, for the Pig Woman and her alarming gap-toothed grin, for her son who was on the point of marrying a nice girl from the next village, for... suddenly Little Li gave a great shout and jumped up. He had the glimmerings of an idea, an idea that might save the villagers. The chieftain, where was the chieftain? He had to find him immediately.

The scribe was in their cave getting ready to grind ink on a stone slab when Little Li burst in and pounded his big fist on the table. "Have you seen the chieftain?" he demanded.

With a sigh the scribe righted the water jar Little Li had knocked over. Mopping the spilled water, he looked with curiosity at the young northerner. "No, I haven't seen him. He's unlikely to be feeling exhilarated at the moment, and I imagine he is in his cave, brooding over means to retrieve the situation." He sighed again. "I doubt there is anything he can do, however."

"Yes, there is!" shouted Little Li. "I've got an idea I have to tell him right away!"

The scribe's eyes narrowed. "What idea?"

"I'll tell you later," said Little Li. "First we have to find the chieftain. He's not in his cave, and Meimei said he left right after dinner. Come on, let's go look for him."

They could not find the chieftain anywhere in the camp, and Little Li became worried. It was growing late, and he did not like the idea of the chieftain wandering alone in his distraught state. He had a more chilling thought: there were men in the outlaw band who wanted to depose the chieftain. Would they go so far as to attack him if they found him alone and defenseless?

Little Li and the scribe separated to comb the hills. As the darkness grew, so did Little Li's anxiety. Remembering the chieftain's stricken face at Master Feng's message, he even considered the possibility that the chieftain might have killed himself in remorse. He had almost given up hope when he came to the waterfall. Above the splashing of the water he heard a sound that made the hair rise at the nape of his neck: laughter, soft, but hysterical and high-pitched. It was not a sound easily forgotten. The phantom in white had appeared again.

Determined this time to capture the phantom, Little Li crept up toward the sound, his soft boots making no noise. He had a great deal of practice in moving silently.

"How does it feel," Little Li heard the voice say, "to have the death of a whole village on your conscience?"

The young outlaw could almost feel the spite in that taunting voice. "You left me to the mercy of the Tartars. Now will you leave the village of Fushan to the mercy of the governor?"

Little Li did not understand the reference to the Tartars, but he knew that the reference to Fushan Village was intended to wound.

"What should I do?" said the chieftain, and there was so much anguish in his voice that Little Li found his own throat tighten painfully. He missed the tormentor's next words, but he heard the last part, ". . . the outlaw band. They are better off under a different leader, wouldn't you say?"

Suddenly Little Li saw it all. This was no ghost in white. This was a cunning human being with a very definite aim: to force the chieftain to resign as the leader of the outlaw band.

With a furious roar, Little Li sprang up and dashed forward to choke off that hateful voice and strike down the diabolical figure in white.

Normally Little Li was surefooted and agile, the result of daily acrobatic training in kung fu. But now he rushed up the hillside in a blind fury. He was dimly aware of crackling underbrush and a flurry of movement above him. In the next instant he crashed into a figure rushing furiously downhill.

Little Li was big, but the other person had the advantage of rushing downhill and consequently having the greater momentum. The young northerner was sent flying. For several seconds he lay winded, while the three-quarter moon and feathery treetops spun in a slow, wide circle above him. Finally he sat up and looked around. Two paces away lay a motionless figure. It stirred, groaned, and slowly sat up. It was the scribe.

Footsteps approached. "And what, may I ask, are you two doing here?" the chieftain asked mildly.

The scribe was the first to recover his voice. "We were looking for you, sir. I saw a figure dressed in a white jacket, and from what I heard of his words, I gathered that his intentions toward you were inimical."

"That fiend!" said Little Li. "I wanted to grab him and—"

"And we met each other instead," finished the scribe. "I'm afraid he succeeded in making his escape."

"Who is he, sir?" asked Little Li. "It seems that he knows you. Is he an old enemy?"

For a long moment the chieftain did not answer. Then he said, in a voice so low that his words were all but inaudible, "He's an old friend."

"I beg to contradict you, sir," said the scribe, "but he did not speak with quite the cordiality of a friend."

"What did he mean about the Tartars, sir?" asked Little Li.

Again there was a long silence. "I'll have to tell you the

whole story," the chieftain said finally. "But first let's go back to the camp. It's very late, and the dampness here is bad for my joints."

After the chieftain had finished telling about the pact he, Old Wu, and Zhang Ru had made in their youth, he looked at the two men sitting across the table from him. They were so young, hardly older than boys—hardly older than he himself had been when he and his friends had taken their vow.

He looked around for Meimei, but she had retired to the bed behind the curtains. When the chieftain, Little Li, and the scribe had entered the cave, she had cooked some thin rice gruel to warm them up after their long exposure to the cold night air.

Little Li dipped the end of one chopstick into a droplet of spilled gruel and idly drew circles. Finally he looked up. "What happened to the third member of your trio, Zhang Ru?" There was a dawning awareness in his eyes, and it was obvious that he suspected a connection between Zhang Ru and the phantom in white.

The chieftain took a deep breath. "He joined the army, and for a while served under my command. But later he was killed in battle."

"Concerning the vow that the three of you took, sir, did you keep faith?" asked the scribe.

The chieftain's eyes fell before those of the scribe. "No, I did not. I broke my vow."

"What happened?" the scribe asked quietly.

Little Li turned fiercely to the scribe. "How can you ask him that? Can't you see how he's suffering?"

The scribe looked only at the chieftain. "What happened?" he repeated. "How did you break faith?"

"We had vowed that we would always help each other," said the chieftain, the words wrenched out of him. "But I didn't help Zhang Ru when he begged me. I left him to the mercy of the Tartars."

Now that he had begun, the rest of the story came out. He saw again that fateful battle—every detail as sharp as if it had taken place yesterday.

The campaign against the Tartars had been going badly. Through court intrigue and envy, Han Baota suspected, supplies and equipment were constantly late in arriving. It was a bitterly cold winter, and the men were downcast despite his efforts to raise their spirits. To cheer them up he had staged martial arts contests and hired troupes of acrobats and players, but to no avail. The soldiers were too cold and too hungry.

Worst of all, he had begun to worry seriously about Zhang Ru. It had become increasingly clear that his friend suffered attacks of panic during battle. His physical courage had never been in doubt when the three friends were young, for they knew that during hunting and weapons practice he was brave to the point of recklessness. But now the men under Zhang Ru had begun to talk, and rumors eventually reached Han Baota. He was aware that some of his orders to Zhang Ru had not been promptly carried out. He had tried to talk to his friend, and had even asked Old Wu to say something, but both had been angrily repulsed.

Then came the calamitous battle with the Tartars. Han Baota never found out why his scouts had not reported the ambush. His task was to save what he could of his army.

The only way, he told Zhang Ru and Old Wu, was to strike through the enemy lines. Retreat was impossible.

Old Wu and his son galloped off to rally what was left of their men. But Zhang Ru remained motionless, although Han Baota shouted at him and shook him by the shoulders. Then Zhang Ru began to giggle. Finally he laughed so hard that he doubled up on his horse. Han Baota's patience snapped. Tight-lipped, he wheeled his horse and rode off to rally his own men.

Later, when he and the Wus had broken through to safety with a few score of their men, a fugitive told them that Zhang Ru had been overtaken by the Tartars. As he was being dragged off his horse, he was heard calling on General Han to remember his vow and help him.

After he had finished his story, the chieftain was afraid to look up. He could not bear to face the contempt of his audience, especially that of Little Li.

But when he finally looked at the two younger men, he saw no contempt. The scribe was merely thoughtful, and Little Li looked deeply moved. He took off his kerchief to mop his eyes, and then blew honkingly into it. "You have no reason to blame yourself, sir," he said huskily. "To save Zhang Ru, you would have had to sacrifice your soldiers."

These were the very words the chieftain had shouted in his own mind, over and over again, as he tried to escape his guilt in abandoning Zhang Ru. Hearing them from Little Li was different. For the first time in four years he could look at himself without flinching.

"I should have seen that Zhang Ru was sick," he insisted. "I should have sent him away and let someone else take over his command, Wu Meng perhaps. But his laughter

infuriated me. So I just rode away and abandoned him."
He felt an almost luxurious pain in probing the deepest part
of his wound.

"You must not blame yourself, sir," repeated Little Li.
"The situation was desperate, and you had no time to worry
about a sick man."

The chieftain felt as if he had been suffering a festering
wound that had just been lanced. The operation had been
excruciating, but now the poison had been drained.

The scribe's voice cut into the chieftain's thoughts. "Are
we to believe that the figure in white is Zhang Ru? That
he had miraculously escaped from the Tartars and has come
back to reproach you?"

"That's who he claims to be," said the chieftain.

"Claims," murmured the scribe. 'You believe, sir, that it
might be someone else?"

"Meimei thinks it may be one of Zhang Ru's offspring,
coming for revenge," said the chieftain.

"Did you see his face, sir?" asked Little Li. "I missed
seeing it both times."

"Tonight his face was hidden by the branches of a tree,"
said the chieftain. "But last time I caught a glimpse."

"Did it look like Zhang Ru?" Little Li asked eagerly.

The chieftain could not suppress a shudder. "No. There
were deep, black holes where his eyes and nose should be.
He said he was mutilated by the Tartars!"

"That's not possible!" the scribe said sharply. "If he had
really lost his eyes, he would not have been able to see his
way in the hills. By the efficient way he escaped us, I would
say his eyesight was excellent."

"But . . . but I saw those ghastly holes!" said the chieftain.

"It was most probably theatrical makeup," said the scribe. "I've seen opera performers with their faces painted in patches of black, or even red, green, and yellow. They looked more like demons than human beings."

The chieftain's shivering gradually stopped and some of the horror left him. What the scribe had said about paint was likely—perhaps it was not even theatrical paint, but just ordinary ink that one could make from rubbing an inkstick on a stone slab.

"Someone is trying to frighten you, sir," said Little Li. "He wants to replace you as the leader of the Tiger Mountain band."

The crushing burden of guilt was back. "Perhaps he's right in wanting to replace me," the chieftain said heavily. "I've brought disaster on the village of Fushan and on this band."

Little Li jumped up. "Not necessarily, sir! I have an idea that might save the village!"

10

✝

A Desperate Plan

Once again the entire band was assembled in the clearing. It was obvious to the chieftain that the mood of the men was altogether different from that of the previous day, when the sky had been dull and overcast, and the meeting, called in the afternoon, had found the men tired and discouraged. The emergency nature of that meeting and the sight of his own haggard face, the chieftain knew, had promoted a feeling of despair.

But this morning the mists that usually surrounded their mountain lair at this time of the year had a luminescence that promised a bright sunny day to come. Moreover, the chieftain had given orders to the cooks at dawn, and into the clearing where they stood came the smell of cooking meat and steaming rice, a sign that there would be a communal feast. The chieftain was well aware that more heartening than anything else was the look on his own face, which expressed hope and determination.

As soon as the men were all present he began. "I've

called you here to discuss a plan for saving the villagers of Fushan." A buzz of excitement arose, and he motioned for silence. "The plan is dangerous and will involve nearly every member of our band. It it fails, we may all be doomed, together with the villagers."

He had to tell them the risks; it would be unfair to conceal the truth. But he had hopes of succeeding, and he knew the men sensed his optimism.

"The idea for this plan came from Little Li," he explained. "He knew that one of the villagers—the son of the Pig Woman, in fact—is supposed to marry a girl from the next village tomorrow."

"But the marriage will certainly be called off, won't it?" asked one of the outlaws. "The relatives of the girl won't want to be allied to a family under sentence of death."

"That's true," admitted the chieftain. "But the news of the sentence on Fushan Village has not necessarily spread. We heard about it only because Master Feng sent us a message. The governor's soldiers have allowed no one out of the village since they occupied it. Of course, they expect the news to leak out gradually; in fact they are counting on it. But officially no one knows about the intended executions yet."

"How does that help us?" demanded a surly voice. The chieftain looked at the speaker and was not particularly surprised to find it was Gao San.

For a moment the chieftain turned and smiled at the Wus and Little Li, who were standing beside him. The four of them had spent most of the night going over the plan. Now Little Li was grinning again like a stone guardian dog, and even Wu Meng's normally grave face was softened by a faint smile. Old Wu had his usual grumpy look, but his eyes were twinkling. When the chieftain turned back to his audience, he saw that they were standing straighter and looking expectant, visibly cheered by the good spirits of their leaders.

"Tomorrow the wedding will go on as scheduled," he told them. "Except that the men of Tiger Mountain will form the bridal party. We will furnish the bride, the bridal attendants, her relatives, and even the hired musicians. We will also deck the bridal sedan chair with special care. The chair will be the largest we can find, because behind the curtains it will contain not only the bride, but also a quantity of weapons."

There were answering smiles from most of the listening outlaws. Even the skeptics, including Gao San and the butcher, had stopped their objections.

"Our plan, of course, is to enter Fushan Village right under the eyes of the soldiers," continued the chieftain, "and create enough of a disturbance to allow the villagers to escape into the hills."

The chieftain's orders were carried out briskly, until it came to the choice of the girl who would act the part of the bride. Suying declared herself the natural candidate. After all, her home was Fushan Village, and her relatives were among the designated victims. It was her solemn duty to play a prominent role in their rescue.

"You're much too weak still," Meimei said. "Most of the attention will be on the bride, and the soldiers especially will be leering and ogling. The bride will need strength and agility to fight her way out during the confusion."

"I don't care!" declared Suying, her lower lip jutting stubbornly. "To free my relatives I'm willing to take any chance!"

"Don't be silly!" snapped Meimei. "It's because of you that we had to buy the medicine and involve the village in the first place. If you're killed during the rescue, everything would be pointless!"

Little Li listened uncomfortably to the exchange between the two girls. He noticed that the chieftain and the Wus had prudently found business elsewhere and had left the cave. He himself had stayed on with a vague notion of giving Suying moral support, but now he had second thoughts. Muttering about an urgent errand, he fled.

Meimei showed a steely strength the young outlaw found somewhat intimidating. He wondered if she was jealous of Suying. Up to now Meimei had been the youngest and by far the most attractive woman in the camp, and her position as the chieftain's mistress had assured her of preeminence. Would this position be challenged by Suying's arrival?

During Suying's illness, Meimei had nursed her with devoted care, Little Li knew. But now the newcomer was up and about, looking around with sparkling eyes. Meimei was no longer the youngest girl present. But she was still the most beautiful since Suying, although attractive in her liveliness, had none of Meimei's fineness of feature.

Meimei had a natural elegance, while Suying had the manners of a village girl. But Suying had spent time as a serving girl in an aristocratic household and must have seen how the rich lived. Perhaps Meimei envied her the experience.

From what Suying had told Little Li, however, he knew

that her experience in the governor's mansion had not been enviable, even before her arrest. Shaking his head, he decided he didn't understand women, especially self-contained women like Meimei. Perhaps he could ask for the opinion of an expert, and he went to look for the scribe.

He found the scribe preparing himself for the role of the leading musician. The musical instruments in a bridal party included gongs, drums, and cymbals, which could be played by anyone willing to listen to the beat. But the bridal procession also included an indispensable instrument called the suona, a double-reed instrument that was not so easy for beginners to play. The scribe had been handed the instrument because he was the only member of the outlaw band who had had any musical training at all. He had protested that his training was in the flute, a refined instrument and very different from the uncouth suona. But Wu Meng had told him brusquely that one wind instrument was much like another, and he had better get busy and learn the fingering.

The scribe's normal style was airy irreverence, but he had learned that it was wise to obey Wu Meng's orders promptly. He got busy, and soon the camp echoed with a gamut of notes, from hoarse squawks to shrill bleats, all of them nasal. He was still hard at work when Little Li approached.

"You sound like a pregnant duck," the young northerner remarked.

The scribe put down the instrument. "Since you're a river man, you probably have a close relationship with pregnant ducks and know what they sound like."

Little Li grinned, squatted down, and picked up the suona and put it to his lips. Even after straining hard, all he could produce was a low *blat*. "This is harder than I thought," he said, surprised.

The scribe grabbed the instrument back. "Of course it's hard. I expended a whole month's supply of saliva on learning to play it." He wiped the reed fastidiously. "See what you've done? The read now smells of garlic!"

Little Li didn't bother to reply. After a moment he said, "Who do you think should be the bride? Meimei or Suying?"

The scribe considered. "It is in the nature of a bride to be shy, modest, and even slightly fearful; therefore it would seem inappropriate for Suying to have the role."

"She would be acting a part," protested Little Li.

"Since you ask my opinion, I should say that playing the part of a shy and retiring girl is beyond Suying's capabilities," said the scribe dryly.

Little Li was still inclined to champion Suying. Then he saw the girl storm out of the cave, and from the look on her face he knew she had lost the argument to Meimei.

"I have to stay behind with a couple of old women," she said bitterly, "while the rest of you go to the village. And Fushan is my own village!"

Little Li tried to comfort her with the promise that she would be on the next raid as soon as her back was healed. But she refused to listen and went off to sulk alone.

Little Li was soon called to help Meimei and several other women decorate the bridal sedan chair. The chair and its furnishings had been supplied by the family of the real bride, who had been glad to cooperate. With his great height, Little Li was assigned the job of hanging ornaments on top of the chair. To protect the bride from the rude gaze of onlookers, the chair was hung with scarlet satin, covered lavishly with embroidery in greens, yellows, gold, and silver. Over the chair went ropes of gold-colored chenille, beads, and baubles. The decorations were in the form of phoenixes, cranes, and all manner of birds and animals auspicious to the occasion.

As he watched Meimei's steady hands and listened to her soft commands, Little Li understood why she had won the argument. Suying might have bluster, but Meimei had determination. Although his devotion had been given to Suying, he became curious about Meimei and watched her unobtrusively. That was how he happened to see her talking quietly to Wu Meng behind the bridal chair while the rest of the women had gone to prepare the evening meal. As their heads bent toward each other, Little Li was struck by a startling resemblance between the two. He had never noticed that before.

Still puzzling over the resemblance, he decided to share his discovery with the scribe and ask his opinion. But first the band had a more important task: saving Fushan Village.

Fushan Village was situated in the foothills of the range that included Tiger Mountain. The village was small, comprising some eight households, plus a few single persons who worked part-time for the more established families. The small size of the village was not unusual in this part of the country, where the soil was too thin and stony for large-scale farming. Nevertheless, Fushan Village was not poor. In addition to working their small plots, the villagers derived additional income from raising animals, such as pigs and chickens. Their most lucrative occupation, however, was cultivating tea. The hills of Anhui were ideal for tea bushes, and the mountainside behind Fushan Village had been planted with tea well beyond the memory of the oldest inhabitant.

Because of the tea, the villagers had found it prudent, even necessary, to be on good terms with the mountain outlaws. The village itself, with its houses, rice paddies, and animal enclosures, was surrounded by a mud wall kept in good repair. But the tea bushes lay outside the wall, some of them a good distance up the hillside. There had always been bands of lawless men in the hills, and the people of Fushan were careful to pay them tribute occasionally: a bale of rice, a side of pork, even some green vegetables.

With the formation of the Tiger Mountain band under the chieftain, the relation between the outlaws and villagers became closer as well as more cordial. For one thing, the chieftain always saw to it that his men paid for all the food they received from the villagers. There was also an understanding that the Tiger Mountain band would protect the village from other marauding bands driven south by the Tartar invasion.

No doubt the governor had long suspected there was collaboration between Fushan Village and the Tiger Mountain men. But without proof he could not summarily arrest the whole village. Provincial governors, after all, had to account for their actions to the emperor. But now the governor had proof: the bolt of silk absolutely identified by the silk merchant. By occupying the village, the governor was striking a devastating blow to the standing of the Tiger Mountain band. He was showing all the other villages in the district how dangerous and unprofitable it was to collaborate with the outlaws.

That was why thirty-six fully armed soldiers now occupied Fushan Village. They patrolled all four walls, making sure no one attempted to climb over and escape. Vigilant guards were mounted over the east and west gates, the only two exits. The governor had given strict orders to permit no one out of the village, however desperate the errand. He had said nothing about allowing anyone in.

The outlaws took a roundabout route, for they had to appear to be coming from the neighboring village. Maneuvering the lavishly decorated bridal sedan through the mountain paths was difficult and several times the chair tipped over. Fortunately, Meimei was not riding in the chair at the time; until they reached flat land she was finding it safer to walk behind the chair. In her elaborate full-skirted costume and high headdress, she had to pick her way carefully to avoid tearing her clothes and ornaments on the tree branches.

The outlaws were relieved when they finally came out of the hills and reached the road running between the two villages. Meimei mounted the sedan chair and the others formed themselves into the appropriate order for a wedding party. Old Wu had been chosen to lead the procession as the father of the bride. As the best actor of the outlaw band, he had the crucial task of convincing the soldiers to admit the wedding party into the village.

Just as they caught sight of Fushan Village in the distance, a voice hailed them and asked them to wait. A bearded figure stepped forward from behind a stand of bamboo. It was Master Feng, and he was holding out a white paper packet.

The chieftain immediately came forward and bowed deeply to Master Feng, thanking him for sending them the warning about the soldiers.

"Yes, yes, I suspected something like this would happen," the hermit said impatiently. "But I haven't come just to hear your thanks." He held out the small paper packet. "I came especially to give you this. It's some medicine for you to give to the pigs. Make sure they take it!"

The chieftain looked bewildered, but he accepted the medicine meekly. Summoning Little Li, he said, "Here, take the medicine and give it to the Pig Boy when you get a chance." Turning to Master Feng, he said, "Naturally we want to help the poor sick pigs, but isn't it more important now to rescue the villagers first?"

But the hermit was already turning away. "The pigs aren't sick," he said curtly over his shoulder. "The medicine will help you with the soldiers."

After Master Feng disappeared into the bamboo again, the wedding party resumed its march toward the village. The musicians began their cacophony, and Little Li soon had his hands full playing the gong. It was not that the gong was at all hard to play—his trouble arose from his disguise. Since he had appeared before the governor during Suying's rescue, he was afraid some of the soldiers occupying Fushan Village might have seen him and would recognize him. With his great height he was conspicuous, as he well knew from his second encounter with the bodyguards. When she learned of his worry, Suying had enthusiastically offered to help with his disguise. She had donated a few locks of her hair, which Little Li had glued to his cheeks, making a bushy beard that hid the lower part of his face. The glue was a gelatinous substance made from pig knuckles, normally used in the camp for binding leather strips to spear shafts and sword handles. Now, as Little Li's face heated with exercise, the glue was softening and he could feel the beard slowly sliding down his jaws. His striking of the gong was constantly interrupted by his need to push his beard back into place. This resulted in the gong being out of beat with the rest of the instruments. The members of the procession had to adjust their steps repeatedly to the music, and soon they began to walk with a curious shuffle.

The scribe stopped blowing his suona and glared at Little Li. "What's wrong with you? Can't you play a simple thing like a gong?"

"It's my beard," mumbled Little Li. As he pushed at the beard again, some of the hair came off his chin and stuck to his fingers. From there the hair passed to the stick and finally to the face of the gong.

"I've never seen a gong in need of a shave before," sputtered the scribe. He tried to control his laughter and resume playing the suona, but he could only produce some hicupping squeaks.

After that the musicians abandoned their efforts to produce music and resigned themselves to simply making noise. At least they succeeded in their function, which was to attract the attention of the soldiers. They saw the west gate of the village swing open and a few soldiers peeking out to investigate.

At a signal from the chieftain, the procession came to a ragged halt some twenty paces from the gate. The music petered out, with the suona ending on a plaintive note, like a lone mandarin duck mourning its mate.

"This is close enough," said the chieftain. "Now we must make them invite us in."

The wedding party broke into small groups, behaving like people puzzled and disconcerted, consulting one another. Meimei even lifted the curtain of her sedan chair and beckoned to one of her female attendants. Several men pointed at the soldiers and shook their heads in dismay, while others nodded vigorously. Little Li pretended to argue with his neighbor.

"I think they're really interested now," said the chieftain. "All right, let's turn around and leave."

"Leave?" exclaimed the butcher. "Aren't we going to the village?"

"Don't be an idiot!" said Gao San. "We're only pretending to leave!"

The musicians picked up their instruments and the bearers picked up the bridal chair. But before the wedding procession could take more than five steps, they heard, "Stop!"

The command came from an officer who was leading a file of ten soldiers out of the gate. The soldiers stopped and leveled their spears at the wedding party.

"Who are you?" demanded the officer. "What are you doing here?"

Old Wu stepped forward. "W-We are the W-Wang family from the next village," he stammered. "M-My daughter is m-marrying Widow He's son today."

The officer turned to his men. "Do you know anything about this?"

One of the soldiers spoke up. "I heard some talk in the village. What he says is true. The Widow He—that's the Pig Woman—is supposed to have a wedding at her home today. I even saw the pile of wedding gifts in her main room."

"The wedding is out of the question now!" snapped the officer.

"Exactly!" Old Wu said eagerly. "So if you'll pardon us for disturbing you, we'll be going immediately."

"Just a moment!" said the officer, his eyes narrowing. "You haven't heard about Fushan Village being occupied?"

"N-No, we've had no word from the village at all," said Old Wu. "Therefore we just assumed the wedding would take place as planned."

The 'bride's mother'—Old Wu's serving woman—pushed herself forward. "What's happened in the village? Has there been a murder?" Her eyes were bright with ghoulish curiosity.

The officer's lips twisted with disdain. "No, nothing interesting like that. We've put the village under arrest for subversive activities."

A buzzing of dismay went through the wedding party. Then the mother of the bride turned to Old Wu. "See? I told you so! I told you not to get mixed up in it!"

"Quiet, you old fool!" shouted Old Wu, shaking her.

"What did she mean?" the officer asked sharply. "What were you mixed up in?"

Old Wu turned a ghastly smile at the officer. "Don't pay any attention to her. She's just upset because the wedding is called off."

It was obvious that the officer was thinking hard: if these

people were mixed up with the outlaws as well, they should be detained for questioning.

The chieftain bustled up. "Of course we didn't know the people in Fushan had anything to do with the outlaws," he said, bowing at the officer with his hands folded in front of him. His hands were trembling visibly. "Otherwise I wouldn't have permitted my niece to be betrothed to the He family."

The officer stared at the chieftain, and after a moment he began to smile grimly. "I said nothing about the outlaws. I only said the village was under arrest for subversive activities."

The chieftain presented a perfect picture of guilt and dismay. "But . . . But . . ."

From inside the sedan chair came a wail. "Under arrest? Does that include my fiancé?"

The curtains parted, and Meimei's head appeared. Brides customarily wore a red silk veil in front of their face, but as if by accident, Meimei brushed against the edge of the curtain and pushed the veil aside, revealing her face. Exquisitely made up, adorned by a headdress sewn with pearls and pieces of jade, she presented a ravishing sight.

The officer's breath hissed, his eyes gleamed, and he began to stroke his mustache. The spears dropped in the hands of the ten soldiers.

Old Wu seemed to notice his 'daughter.' "Cover yourself, you shameless girl!" he cried, twitching close the curtains of the sedan chair. Turning to the officer, he bowed. "We must not waste any more of your time. Since the affairs of Fushan Village no longer concern us, we'll return immediately to our village."

He seemed in a great hurry to leave. The bearers picked up the bridal chair.

The officer came to himself with a start. He barked a curt order to his men, who spread out on both sides of the wedding party and pointed their spears.

"You will not be returning to your village until I have asked you some questions," the officer said coldly.

There was nothing for the wedding party to do but bow to authority and meekly follow the officer through the gate into Fushan Village.

11

The Escape of the Villagers

When the Pig Woman and her son opened their gate and were confronted with the wedding party, they were struck dumb with amazement. It was just as well, for the Pig Woman recognized Little Li in spite of his molting beard, and would have blurted out something revealing. As it was, she could only gape and show her four teeth.

Old Wu broke the silence. "I know that it's not the custom for the bride's family to enter the house of her future husband during the wedding, but we were not given any choice in the matter."

Mother and son stared glassily a few moments longer, and then comprehension finally appeared in their eyes. The Pig Woman closed her mouth, swallowed, and managed a bow. "You . . . you are still willing to give us your daughter?"

Old Wu smiled ruefully. "We didn't hear anything about your . . . uh . . . misfortune, and we just went ahead with the wedding as planned." He turned and indicated the soldiers. "This officer ordered us to accompany him to your house."

The son was making an effort to collect his wits. "Yes, well, things are not normal here, and we'd given up on the wedding, to tell the truth." He looked around distractedly.

The chieftain stepped forward and cleared his throat. "I don't suppose you've prepared a wedding feast either. No food or wine?"

At the mention of food and wine, the soldiers in the courtyard stirred restlessly, and even the officer's nose twitched.

The Pig Woman was a faster thinker than her son. "My neighbors were helping me with the preparations for the feast," she said. "Of course everything came to a stop when the soldiers occupied our village."

The officer and his men looked at one another and a common thought was obviously running through their minds: after their second full day of depressing guard duty over Fushan Village, they deserved some reward. What food they had eaten had been grudgingly prepared by the villagers and served in an atmosphere of sullen resentment. If the wedding feast were allowed to proceed, there would be prospect of decent food at last. Perhaps they could have some fun with the bride and her attendants at the feast. They could even bring in a few of the village girls.

"Very well," said the officer. He turned to the Pig Woman's son. "Go tell your neighbors to get busy and prepare the wedding feast as originally planned. And tell them to hurry!"

"The bride's family wasn't supposed to attend the feast," objected the Pig Woman. "The least you can do is have them make themselves useful. How about asking some of the young fellows there to help carry firewood?"

The officer saw nothing wrong with the suggestion. He

waved his hand at the younger members of the wedding party. "You heard what the Pig...uh...Widow He said. Go and get some firewood."

The chieftain gave an almost imperceptible nod. Little Li, the scribe, Gao San, and the butcher detached themselves and followed the Pig Boy into the main street of the village.

Little Li issued his instructions quickly. "Tell all the people to collect their valuables and be ready to leave when we give the signal," he told the Pig Boy.

"Tell them not to bring any large pieces of furniture, like a clothes chest," added Gao San. "We have to be able to run quickly!"

The Pig Boy nodded. "What's the signal?" he asked.

"The signal will be the gong," replied Little Li. "When you hear the gong being struck quickly and loudly, head for the gates."

"I've just thought of something," said the Pig Boy. "There is a place in the south wall that's weak. Maybe we can break through there. The guards won't be watching the walls as carefully as the gates."

"I thought all the walls of the village were in good shape," said Little Li.

"This just happened the day before yesterday," said the Pig Boy. "Fat Liu was unloading some buckets of fertilizer, and his cart slipped and crashed into the wall. We helped him patch up the crack, but the mud is still wet over that part and it's not hardened yet." He looked at Little Li's husky frame. "Someone like you could easily break down the weak part."

The chieftain had ordered everyone to go through the gates, and he liked to have all the details of an expedition meticulously planned ahead, but this was too good an opportunity to miss. "All right," said Little Li. "Tell the people to rush for the breach in the wall at the signal."

"What about the soldiers?" asked the Pig Boy. "One of them might spot us going over and give the alarm."

"We'll keep the soldiers busy," said Little Li. "You just make sure that old women, children, and other slower people get through first."

Just as the Pig Boy was turning away, Little Li remembered something and called him back. "Here is some medicine that Master Feng wants you to feed your pigs."

Puzzled, the Pig Boy took the small paper packet. "Why does he want to give the pigs medicine? They're not sick."

"I don't know either," admitted Little Li. "But he was very insistent about giving it to them. He said it would help us with the soldiers."

Gao San was frowning as he watched the Pig Boy speed off to inform the villagers of the escape plan. "I don't see why we have to burden ourselves with the old and the feeble of the village," he grumbled. "They're just so many more useless mouths to feed."

"The chieftain made it very clear that we must try to save everyone," Little Li told him.

"That's foolish!" said Gao San. "The welfare of our band comes first! The village weaklings will slow us down!"

The scribe stared contemptuously at Gao San. "I believe the chieftain considers it his duty to secure the safety of everyone under his protection. That's what makes him a true leader instead of just a petty thief."

At the scribe's words Gao San clenched his fists. "Are you calling me a petty thief?"

Before the scribe could reply, Little Li stepped between the two men. "We've got enough to do without squabbling among ourselves," he told Gao San. "Why don't you go get some firewood? The soldiers will be suspicious if we return empty-handed. And when you're finished, you'd better go back and tell the chieftain about the change of plans."

As Gao San and the butcher went off for firewood, Little Li looked at them anxiously, disturbed by their readiness to defy the chieftain's orders. He hadn't forgotten the near mutiny back at the outlaw camp, when a faction under Gao San had been ready to depose the chieftain. "Do you realize something?" he said uneasily. "Our whole band is here in the village and we are outnumbered by the soldiers. Our only advantage is surprise. What if someone warns the soldiers of our plan?"

"That's occurred to me also," said the scribe. His normally pale face was slightly flushed, and Little Li had the strange feeling that he looked uncomfortable. "If one of us is a traitor," muttered the scribe, "this would be his chance to bring about the destruction of the whole band."

A hideous thought suddenly occurred to Little Li: "The phantom in white—*could he be one of us?* If he's working for the governor, this whole expedition could turn out to be a huge trap. We'll be lucky to fight our way out, much less save the villagers!"

The scribe was silent for a moment. When he spoke again, his voice had regained its normal carelessness. "I don't believe we have to concern ourselves with the phantom in white for the moment. Shall we go and inspect the breach in the wall?"

According to the Pig Boy, the weak part was in the south wall. This was an advantage, since the south side of the village faced the mountains and the fugitives would find it easier to escape into the hills.

Little Li and the scribe picked up some firewood at two of the farmhouses while looking at the south wall across a row of vegetable plots. They could see four soldiers pacing alongside the wall, apparently to prevent any attempt to scale it. A large dark patch, where the mud was wet, marked the portion of the wall that was newly mended. After the soldiers had passed, the two outlaws sauntered casually past the vegetable plots for a closer look at the mended patch.

"What a stench!" said the scribe. "How do the farmers stand it?"

"It's the fertilizer," said Little Li. "Farmers use human waste. You've led a pampered life in the city, so you wouldn't know about it."

But as they approached, even Little Li had to admit that the smell was overpowering. He put his scarf over his nose and mouth. "I remember now. The Pig Boy said that a fertilizer cart crashed into the wall. Some of the fertilizer must have spilled out."

"At least the soldiers wouldn't be likely to linger around here," said the scribe in a muffled voice, covering his nose and mouth with his hands. "We've seen enough. Let's go back to the others."

* * *

The chieftain watched in admiration as Old Wu allowed himself to be squeezed dry of information drop by slow drop. Gradually it became evident to even the most stupid soldier present that what Old Wu was saying about the activities of the Fushan villagers was confused, improbable, and self-contradictory. The officer's face grew red with anger. "Lies! You're telling me lies! Do you expect me to believe that the bandits come here every day to feast with the villagers?"

Old Wu looked desperately anxious to please. "I'm just telling you what you want to hear—rumors of what goes on in this village."

"I don't want rumors!" roared the officer. "I want facts!"

"But I don't know any facts," said Old Wu, shrinking back. "All I can tell you is hearsay."

The chieftain judged that enough time had passed for all the villagers of Fushan to have learned of the escape plan. By now they should be gathering up their belongings and tying them into bundles. When Little Li struck the gong, the villagers should be ready to rush for one of the two gates. Half of the outlaws, under the Wus, would be at the east gate to protect the villagers leaving that way. The rest, under himself and Little Li, would be at the west gate.

Where was Little Li? It was almost time for him to return and strike the gong. From the officer's exasperation, Old Wu would not be able to drag out the interrogation much longer. The chieftain and Old Wu were being questioned by the officer in the central room of the Pig Woman's house. The bridal sedan chair and the rest of the party were outside in the courtyard, guarded by a dozen soldiers. The chieftain could hear voices raised outside, and occasionally a burst of laughter from the soldiers. He was worried about the increasing raucousness of the laughter.

Where was Little Li? he thought again. It was time to give the signal. Surely the villagers should be ready to move by now.

Suddenly the chieftain heard a tearing of cloth, followed by a scream. He started up and headed for the door, but was prevented from leaving by two of the soldiers crossing their spears in front of him. But he could see what was happening in the courtyard, and the sight dismayed him.

Two of the soldiers, impatient with the long wait, had pulled Meimei out of the sedan chair. One of them had his arms around her waist, and the other one had just ripped off the embroidered panels of her skirt, exposing her long trousers underneath. Meimei was not the one who had screamed, however. That was one of the other girls, fighting off a soldier who had his hands on her breast.

With a lithe twist, Meimei tore herself free from the man holding her, turned, and aimed a vicious kick at his stomach. The soldier doubled over in agony. She was already whirling around to strike the other soldier, the one who had ripped her skirt. She chopped him on the neck with the edge of her hand, and he fell soundlessly.

The chieftain winced. He knew Meimei could fight, having seen her at practice with the monk. But it was disconcerting all the same to see this display of cold efficient martial skill in the girl who attended him every night.

He also knew that Meimei's actions had precipitated the fight prematurely, before Little Li had given his signal. But it was too late to stop it now. Sighing, the chieftain pushed up his sleeves and with a sudden jerk seized a spear from one of the soldiers standing in front of him. Busy watching Meimei, the man was caught unawares.

Little Li heard the sounds of fighting even before reaching the Pig Woman's house. "That's funny! They've started without waiting for me to give the signal."

"Perhaps the officer grew suspicious and forced the chieftain's hand," said the scribe. They began to run.

They found the courtyard boiling with confusion. Most of the outlaws had managed to find a weapon from the sedan chair and were beating back the soldiers. The clash of weapons could also be heard from inside the house. Little Li couldn't see the chieftain or Meimei, but he did see Gao San.

"Did you tell the chieftain about the new plan?" Little Li asked. "About going through the gap in the wall instead of through the gates?"

Gao San sent an attacking soldier reeling back. His character might not be of the highest, but he was a good fighter. "I couldn't get to the chieftain," he panted, "but I told Wu Meng, and he said he would tell him."

Little Li was relieved. If Wu Meng knew about the change of plans, he would make sure the chieftain was informed. The young northerner fought his way to the corner of the courtyard where he had left his gong. The stick for beating the gong had disappeared, but a piece of firewood served instead. Raising his arm high, he began to strike the gong with all his might. So reverberating was the gong that a lull in the fighting settled for a moment over the whole courtyard as everyone turned to stare. Then the combatants fell to work again.

The villagers should all have heard the signal by now, thought Little Li, putting down the gong. It was time for him to head for the breach in the wall, where the villagers would soon be gathering.

The next instant he was chilled by a piercing scream. Two more screams followed, so ghastly that he couldn't see how a human throat could have produced them. Then he realized they were not produced by humans: they were squeals coming from pigs.

There was a sudden rush, and Little Li was nearly trampled by his fellow outlaws pushing past him and out the gate of the Pig Woman's residence. Someone seized him by the arm.

"What are you waiting for?" cried the scribe, pulling Little Li after him. Once outside the gate, they slammed it after them. Using pieces of firewood, they wedged the gate closed.

Little Li saw that his companion looked shaken. "It's . . . It's Master Feng's medicine," stammered the scribe. "It drove the pigs wild."

From inside the courtyard came dreadful grunts and squeals and the whimpering of terrified soldiers. "How many soldiers are still trapped there?" asked Little Li.

"About a dozen," said the scribe. "They won't be fit for much by the time the pigs quiet down again."

Once they saw the face of a frantic soldier as the man tried to climb over the fence. Then he yelped and fell back as something attacked him from behind.

The scribe grimaced. "I don't think I shall ever be able to face a dish of pork again."

"Never mind the pork!" said Little Li. "Let's go to the south wall. The chieftain and the others should be there by now."

Twilight was the traditional time for a wedding, a custom that had not been forgotten by the chieftain when he planned the expedition. The sun had been low when the wedding party reached Fushan Village. Now, as Little Li and the scribe raced for the south wall, leaving a household of terrified soldiers and hysterical pigs, it was growing dark. That made it harder for the rest of the soldiers guarding Fushan to see the movement of the villagers.

By now the soldiers probably realized something was happening in the Pig Woman's house, and they might come to investigate. They might even suspect that a few of the villagers would make an attempt to escape. In that case, the guards at the two gates would be reinforced, reducing the number of men watching the walls.

"My nose informs me that we are getting close," said the scribe.

The stench of the spilled fertilizer was unmistakable, but as they approached the south wall, Little Li forgot about the smell when he saw that the evacuation of the villagers had already started. Someone had made a wide breach in the wall and the villagers, carrying their cloth bundles, were passing through the gap in an orderly fashion. Although they were moving quickly, they showed no signs of panic. The outlaws formed a protective ring about them, and the few soldiers coming to investigate were easily kept at bay.

More soldiers were arriving, however. Little Li felt a movement behind him and swerved just in time to avoid the lunge of a spearman. Missing the young outlaw, the soldier stepped on something soft—what it was Little Li preferred not to know—and skidded to his knees. Little Li wrested the spear from the soldier and stunned its owner with a neat blow.

Armed with the spear, the young outlaw easily beat back two more soldiers who had arrived to investigate the reason for the crowd. It wouldn't be long, thought Little Li, before more soldiers came. But meanwhile the evacuation was proceeding smoothly, and it looked as if the villagers would escape in time. All that remained was for the outlaws to fight a rearguard action.

"Something is wrong," a voice said at Little Li's elbow. It was the scribe, armed with a stick of firewood and looking worried. "Not all of our men are here."

Fewer soldiers were arriving, and Little Li was able to spare a moment for a count of the outlaws. The scribe was right. Most of the outlaws were here, it was true, but at least a quarter of the men were missing. Could so many of their comrades have fallen as casualties?

The scribe's next words were even more ominous. "I don't see the chieftain anywhere."

Little Li's heart missed a beat. He looked frantically at the ring of outlaws protecting the villagers. He saw the two Wus and also Meimei, who was helping an old woman step past a fallen soldier. But nowhere could he see the slight figure of the chieftain. The moon was up and it was nearly full, giving enough light for recognizing faces. With growing dismay, Little Li saw that as well as the chieftain several others of the veterans most loyal to the chieftain were missing.

"I wonder if the chieftain could still be at the west gate," said the scribe, frowning.

"Why should he be?" snapped Little Li, his voice sharp with worry. "Gao San said he told Wu Meng about the change of plans!"

"That doesn't mean the chieftain got the message," the scribe said slowly.

"Come on, we'd better go to the west gate," said Little Li.

They could hear a growing noise as they ran toward the western end of the village. Little Li realized that the reason why fewer soldiers were going to the south wall was because most of them were rushing over to investigate the uproar at the west gate.

As Little Li and the scribe arrived at the gate, they found their worst fears realized. Fighting desperately with their backs to the gate were the chieftain and five other outlaws. They were nearly surrounded by at least twenty soldiers, and it was clear that they would shortly be overwhelmed.

With a savage yell, Little Li twirled his spear above his head and leaped into the fight. His huge size and ferocity scattered the soldiers, and before they could press forward again he dashed his way to the chieftain.

The chieftain was nearly spent, and as Little Li reached him he lowered his sword and tottered.

"Are you wounded, sir?" cried Little Li, putting out his arm to support the chieftain.

"No, just tired," panted the chieftain. Catching a sobbing breath he asked, "Where are the villagers? I heard your gong. Why didn't they move?"

Little Li was just opening his mouth to answer when he heard someone cry, "Look out!" He turned, but it was already too late. A sword was slashing down at him.

At the last possible moment the sword seemed to swerve. It missed him by so little that he felt a breeze against his cheek. Raising his spear to face his attacker, he saw that the soldier was already engaged with another opponent. To Little Li's amazement, he realized that the soldier's opponent was the scribe. It was the scribe's intervention that had saved him from the soldier's slash.

The scribe was still armed with his stick of firewood, and Little Li noticed that he was holding it in an unexpectedly competent manner. Perhaps all those lessons with Wu Meng had taken effect, although they had seemed utterly futile at the time.

The soldier bared his teeth and lunged viciously with his sword. The scribe pivoted on his heel, narrowly escaping the lunge, and swung his stick at his opponent's ribs. The soldier dropped his sword with a groan.

This time Little Li no longer had any doubts: the scribe was an experienced fighter with a stick. But he had no time to ponder over this curious fact, for he was attacked on both sides by two other soldiers. For a time Little Li and his spear were kept fully occupied protecting the chieftain.

The arrival of Little Li and the scribe had given a temporary respite to the small beleaguered band of outlaws at the west gate, but they were still hopelessly outnumbered. Even the young northerner was beginning to tire after a while. The villagers should have all left by now, he thought. Would Old Wu or Wu Meng notice that the chieftain and some of the others were missing and come looking for them?

In the end they were saved by their enemy. A voice was yelling in the distance, and a figure came running whom Little Li recognized as the officer commanding the troops in Fushan Village. His uniform showed signs of wear, whether from engagements with the outlaws or with pigs it was not clear.

"You idiots!" he shouted furiously at his soldiers. "What are you doing here? The villagers are all escaping through a gap in the south wall!"

Shocked, the soldiers at the west gate lowered their weapons and one by one began to turn toward the southern part of the village. The officer lashed them on with his voice. "After them! We may still catch them before they all escape into the hills!"

After the soldiers had run off, the chieftain looked at Little Li in bewilderment. "Is this true? Have the villagers really escaped through a hole in the south wall?"

"I thought you knew," said Little Li. "The rest of our men were at the gap, covering the villagers' escape."

"No, I didn't . . ." the chieftain began.

But he was interrupted by the scribe. "We'd better escape ourselves before any of the soldiers return." His voice sounded fainter than usual.

Little Li pushed open the west gate and the outlaws started forward. But they were not the first ones through the gate. With a snort and a squeal, a bulky shape rushed out of the darkness, knocked the scribe off his feet, and streaked through the gate. The rustling sound of its passage through the bushes gradually died away.

Little Li began to laugh, but stopped when he saw that the scribe was getting up very slowly and painfully. "Did you hurt yourself?" he asked.

The scribe clenched his teeth. "No, I did not hurt myself. There were plenty of soldiers who were willing to do it for me."

Then Little Li saw what he had been too busy to notice before: the front of the scribe's jacket was dark with blood. "You're wounded!" he exclaimed.

"A natural consequence of bare steel meeting bare flesh," said the scribe. "But it's not a deep cut, and I can manage to reach home, if I'm not assaulted by any more pigs."

In addition to the scribe, six other outlaws had sustained various cuts and bruises. Most of them were among the little group fighting at the west gate.

The soldiers, under their furious officer, attempted to pursue the villagers, but they were hampered by darkness. They were also unfamiliar with the mountain paths, which the outlaws knew intimately.

A portion of the outlaw band were assigned the task of guiding the villagers, while the rest were ordered to harry and delay the soldiers. By dawn, the last of the villagers of Fushan had reached the hideout safely.

12

十二

The Scribe's Confession

With the addition of the Fushan villagers, the character of the outlaw band changed. No longer could they call themselves the Brothers of Tiger Mountain, since some half of the villagers were women, bringing the total number of women in the camp to nearly thirty. The harsh atmosphere of a predominantly male camp was being modified by the sound of female voices and the laughter and bawling of children.

There were even animal sounds. The Pig Woman and her son had managed to round up a few of their animals. After the effect of Master Feng's drug had worn off, the pigs had become abnormally docile and were easily driven.

Shelter for the people and animals was the most immediate task. Fortunately, the new arrivals included a number of skillful craftsmen, and soon the mountainside echoed with the sound of axes and saws. Timber was all around them. Although there was no time to season the wood, the freshly felled trees provided fragrant lumber good enough for the temporary buildings that would house them over the winter.

The veteran outlaws and the new arrivals worked together in a spirit of cooperation. Later there might be bickering between the two groups and adjustments to be made, but for the time being the activities suggested preparations for a festival. Indeed, a feast was being planned to celebrate the union of the two groups into a new community.

Lacking skills in carpentry, Little Li was more usefully employed carrying logs. In his enthusiasm he soon carried more than enough to keep the carpenters busy. Although the camp was noisy and bristling with activity, Little Li felt slightly lonely. He had not been able to exchange more than a few dozen words with Suying since the arrival of the villagers. She was an orphan, for both her parents were dead, but she had friends and cousins among the new arrivals, and she spent most of her time eagerly listening to news about her former home. Always surrounded by a circle of her old friends, she had no time to talk to Little Li. She was far too busy catching up on village happenings, and after hearing all the news, she had lost no time telling about her own adventures. Judging by the exclamations of horror from her listeners, Little Li guessed she was painting a vivid picture of her ordeal at the hands of the governor's jailers. If she could speak so freely of the experience, it meant at least her wounds must have healed.

And that reminded Little Li of the scribe, whom he had not seen since their return. He had some questions for the young scholar. Together with the other wounded, the scribe had been placed in a cave under the care of Master Feng.

But when Little Li arrived at the cave, he found the scribe already gone.

At Little Li's question, Master Feng said irritably, "I sent him away. He was healing nicely, and besides, he talked so much that he disturbed my other patients."

The scribe was watching the construction of a new pigpen with all the fascination of a city boy who had never been close to animals. When he saw Little Li approach, he sighed. "I know, it's time for me to carry water again."

Little Li had less patience than usual with the scribe's flippancy. "You can drop your act now," he said grimly. "I want to have a talk with you."

They walked off into the trees until the noise of the camp was just an indistinct murmur. The scribe looked sidelong at his companion. "You'll be disappointed. Underneath my mask of a lazy dilettante, you'll find another lazy dilettante."

Little Li pointed at a rock. "Sit down!" When the other man was seated, he said, "First of all, tell me why you pretended all these weeks to be hopeless at martial exercises. I saw you handle that stick back at Fushan Village. You've had lessons before, probably very intensive lessons."

The scribe merely grinned. "I only wanted to inject a little good humor into the camp, since our morale had become so lamentably low. Think of all the hours of entertainment I gave to Gao San, the butcher, and all the other spectators."

"You overdid it," Little Li said sourly. "I got suspicious because you didn't even try to defend yourself."

"I was afraid that if I resisted, my reflexes would take over," explained the scribe. "The monk or Wu Meng would have known I was too well-trained for someone of my scholarly background."

"Are you working for the governor?" Little Li asked bluntly.

For once the scribe's answer was short. "I was."

Little Li's anger burst out. He seized the scribe by the shoulders and shook him furiously. "You treacherous snake! After we took you in and accepted you as one of us!"

A gasp escaped the scribe and he turned pale. Little Li suddenly remembered that the other man had been wounded. He dropped his hands. "Sorry, I forgot," he muttered.

The scribe took a deep breath and recovered some of his color. "It wasn't a deep cut anyway, although I hardly think your massage is the recommended treatment for it."

Little Li's anger was fading. He thought over the scribe's actions in Fushan Village and found himself perplexed. If the scribe were really working for the governor, why hadn't he betrayed them to the soldiers? The whole outlaw band could have been captured.

"All right, you'd better tell me the whole story," he said.

The scribe was silent for a moment, and then he sighed. "I had hoped my actions would speak for themselves, but I should have known that sooner or later I would have to tell you the truth."

"Then it's true?" demanded Little Li, feeling a keen regret despite himself. "You really work for the governor?"

"I *was* working for the governor," corrected the scribe. "I don't anymore. If you doubt me, think of all the opportunities I have had for betraying you. When you and Wu Meng were in the governor's palace rescuing Suying, I was also in the city, and I could have told the authorities who you were. And wouldn't you say that in Fushan Village I was fighting on your side?"

"That's what I don't understand," said Little Li. "What made you change sides?"

"What made me change sides was the character of your chieftain," the scribe said slowly. "I admired his methodical planning and his attention to details. But most of all I was deeply impressed by his humanity. He cared for all of us as if we were his children. Can you guess at what precise moment I gave him my loyalty?"

Little Li thought for a moment, and suddenly he knew. "It was when he insisted on buying the medicine for Suying in spite of the risks, wasn't it?"

The scribe nodded. "Your chieftain truly cared about the people under his protection." He added bitterly, "*He* should be the governor of this province, not that lecher in the city!"

Little Li noticed that the scribe could not speak of the governor without loathing. "If you hate the governor so much, why did you work for him?" he asked.

The scribe looked away. Then he said abruptly, "I needed money."

Little Li's anger returned. "Don't lie to me! Your family must be rich! Since your sister is the governor's favorite, she should be able to shower you with money!"

At the mention of his sister, the scribe turned sharply to look at Little Li. But instead of replying, he looked away again.

And then Little Li saw an inkling of the truth. "You needed money for your sister, didn't you? Why?"

The scribe's mouth twisted. "You've seen the governor, and you can imagine the sort of man he is. What do you think it's like to be married to him?"

"What were you planning to do?" asked Little Li.

"My sister was originally betrothed to another man," said the scribe. "I was hoping that if I gave her enough money she could still marry him, instead of becoming one of the governor's secondary wives."

Little Li did not understand. "If the betrothal was all set up, why didn't your sister marry her fiancé? Why do you need more money?"

The scribe frowned impatiently. "You probably think that anyone who reads and writes can afford to wear silk clothes and eat from china bowls and has no money problems?"

That was in fact what Little Li did think. "What broke up the engagement, then?" he asked.

"I told you already: money," said the scribe. "Our family used to be wealthy, because my father was an official. But after my mother died, my father lost interest in his career and decided to lead a retired life. He not only gave up his position, he cut himself off from society."

It would be like losing both parents at once, thought Little Li. He could sympathize, for he had also lost his family. "How old were you then?" he asked.

"I was sixteen," said the scribe. "That was three years ago." That meant that despite his worldly airs, the scribe was nineteen years old, only a year older than Little Li. "My sister is two years younger than I am, but in many ways she's more mature. She encouraged me to continue my studies, and she tried to take the place of our mother." His voice broke a little.

Little Li felt his own throat tighten. He was touched by the picture of a fourteen-year-old girl assuming maternal airs and trying to raise the morale of her brother.

The scribe cleared his throat and continued. "After my father retired, our family affairs were managed by a relative. To this day I don't know if he cheated us deliberately or simply mismanaged. In any case, the result was that when it came time for my sister's wedding, we discovered we could not pay for the costly gifts to the groom's family that were part of the marriage agreement."

"I see," said Little Li. "So the money you needed was for the marriage gifts."

The scribe nodded. "I heard that a huge reward was being offered for the capture of the Tiger Mountain outlaws. I approached the officer in charge of the campaign against the outlaws and offered to join the outlaw band as a spy for the governor."

"Was that about the time we were planning to raid the money box?" asked Little Li.

"No, it was several weeks earlier," said the scribe. "The man who recruited me thought I should have an intensive course in hand-to-hand combat in case I was found out and needed to escape."

"I knew you'd already been trained!" said Little Li.

"Actually, I'd had earlier lessons as well, since my father believed in a balanced education," said the scribe. "For this intensive training course I had to go away to a monastery outside of the city. The officer thought it wise to keep the project a secret. We didn't know about Suying at the time, but he was sure your outlaw band had a spy in the city."

"You didn't tell your sister what you were going to do?" asked Little Li.

"No! She would have tried to stop me. I told her I was joining the army. It sounded less risky and less—dishonorable."

The scribe stopped speaking, and for a minute they could hear the distant noise of the camp's activities, like the chattering of birds.

When he resumed his story, the scribe's expression was stark. "I returned to the city and found that my relative had arranged for my sister to be married to the governor as his third wife. Since she would not be a principal wife, the marriage would not cost my relative any money."

"You were too late to stop the marriage?" asked Little Li.

The scribe nodded. "She had already entered the governor's household. At first I still had hopes of getting her away. That was why I went ahead with the plan to join your band. Afterward I heard she had become a favorite, and I thought she might feel content, or at least secure. And then Suying said she looked unhappy . . ."

Little Li tried to think of something comforting to say. "Maybe Suying just happened to see your sister when she was out of sorts," he said. "Her life is probably quite luxurious. I'm sure she doesn't have to carry water, for instance."

There was no response from the scribe. When Little Li left him, he was sitting with his head bowed, staring at his hands.

* * *

Little Li was relieved that his suspicions about the scribe had been cleared. He liked the young scholar, who was proving to be a valuable addition to the band. He had shown he could think quickly and move quickly when necessary. Little Li was glad he had not turned out to be the traitor.

But that meant someone else was. Someone else was the phantom in white; someone else had taken the money from the money box while he left it unguarded. Was the phantom an agent of the governor? Since the scribe had been the governor's spy, he would likely have known if the phantom had been sent as a fellow agent. Therefore Little Li had to admit that the phantom was not the governor's man, but a member of the outlaw band. It was someone whose purpose was to destroy the chieftain's peace of mind, to force him to resign as the leader. In other words, it was a plot by someone anxious to assume leadership.

Who it was, Little Li thought he knew. But he shrank from his suspicion—he did not want to believe that Wu Meng was the guilty one. Yet however much he tried, he could not forget that during the attack in Fushan Village, the chieftain had not learned of the change in plans, although Gao San had told Wu Meng. As a consequence, the chieftain had nearly lost his life.

Wu Meng was the man the young northerner had always taken as his model. His fighting skills, coolness, resourcefulness, and courage were all the qualities Little Li admired the most. It wrenched his heart to think that a man of Wu Meng's apparent nobility could be capable of such treachery.

Little Li walked slowly back to the camp, wondering how he could warn the chieftain. Old Wu and the chieftain had been friends since childhood, and the news of Wu Meng's betrayal would hurt him deeply. Furthermore, would the chieftain even believe him?

There was another difficulty, perhaps even more crucial. Suppose Wu Meng were unmasked as the betrayer of the chieftain; might not some of the outlaws choose to side with him? It was obvious how Gao San and the butcher would stand. Of the men who could be counted on as loyal to the chieftain, Little Li was sure only of himself, the monk, the small handful of men who had fought with them at the west gate of Fushan, and the scribe. Of the others, perhaps a majority would prefer a younger, more vigorous, more dashing leader. That was the sort of leader Little Li himself would have liked, but not if he had risen through treachery.

Deeply troubled and unhappy, Little Li arrived back at the camp, where the first people he saw were Wu Meng and Meimei, deep in conversation. Again Little Li was struck by how alike they were—the same wide brows, short straight nose, and high cheekbones. Wu Meng did not resemble his father at all, but he and Meimei were as like as brother and sister.

Was even Meimei loyal to the chieftain? Little Li decided sadly that he could not be sure. As for her resemblance to Wu Meng, he could not explain it; nor could he see what it had to do with the phantom in white.

The feasting lasted until late. Even the children were allowed to join the banquet, seated at a little square table of their own and handed food by their parents. The food was lavish and more delicious than the outlaw band had tasted for years. They ate rice, unadulterated with millet or any of the lesser grains. They had ham and salted fish, and delicacies rescued from the Pig Boy's postponed wedding feast. The outlaws brought out their choicest foods from storage, and the villagers contributed generously from their supplies. Later the chieftain would have to consult someone from the village on keeping an eye on supplies and rationing, but tonight all feasted without restraint, celebrating the success of the rescue and the beginning of a new life for the villagers.

Eight big square tables, several of them just fashioned by the newly arrived carpenters, had been set out for the banquet under the trees. The air was not too cold for outdoor feasting, although the colder weather would soon come. Seated at the chieftain's table was the village elder. After exchanging toasts with the elder, the chieftain rose and visited the other tables in turn, toasting the new arrivals at each one. The women, of course, sat at their own tables, where Meimei acted as the chieftain's hostess.

The chieftain, who made a point of observing everything, noticed that Suying glanced repeatedly at the table at which the younger outlaws were sitting. She had been eyeing the scribe with unmistakable admiration. The scribe, however, seemed disconcerted by the girl's forwardness. To complicate matters, Little Li was apparently smitten by Suying. The chieftain sighed a little. There was potential for unhappiness here, but he hoped a happy solution could be found for the three young people. Since her rescue, Suying had become accustomed to too much freedom in the outlaw camp. Fortunately, the arrival of her older relatives from Fushan Village put a check on her.

Looking at the chattering company around him, the chieftain knew that his prestige had never been higher with his men. The rescue of the villagers right under the noses of a troop of government soldiers had been a masterly operation that had enhanced the reputation of the Tiger Mountain men throughout the district. For many miles around the peasants would know that the outlaws considered it their duty to protect the people from the soldiers and had the power to do so.

Flushed with wine, the chieftain returned smiling to his own table. As he was sitting down, the warmth from the wine suddenly drained from his face and he was overtaken by a shudder. The evening had been a personal triumph for him, but this very triumph had placed him in danger. His enemy, the phantom in white, had been content so far to taunt him and attempt to break his spirit. But his spirit had not broken: it had soared with the success of the Fushan expedition. Therefore the enemy would have to go further. The chieftain was certain the phantom would now attack him physically—attack with intent to murder.

The chieftain pretended to have drunk more wine than he actually had. While continuing to toast his guests and to accept toasts, he had taken only sips of the hot wine and had tried to empty his cup on the ground whenever possible. As he laughed and responded to congratulations and jests, this seemed one of the longest evenings he had ever spent.

But at last the feast was over and the guests retired to their shelters. The chieftain returned to his cave, rinsed his face with cold water, and sat down to think about what he should do. He was resolved on one thing: he would not cower in fear and look constantly over his shoulder, waiting for an attack.

Suddenly his mind was made up. In war one could never win by waiting for an attack and then trying to devise some method of defense. It was better to go out and meet the enemy. He knew, of course, where he would find his enemy: at the waterfall, his favorite place for seeking peace and quiet. Somehow his enemy had discovered this, and by spying on him always knew when he took his walk there in the evening. Very well, then, he would meet the phantom in white one more time by the waterfall, but this time he would be armed.

As the chieftain was picking up his sword, Meimei returned to the cave. She had been storing away the leftover food and cleaning up after the banquet with the other women of the camp. She looked tired, but she greeted him in her usual soft, gentle voice. Her eyes widened when she saw his sword.

An idea came to the chieftain. He was not a good swordsman; he never had been, and the growing stiffness of his joints had not improved his technique. In a sword duel with his enemy, he had little hope of winning. There was a better weapon available to him. Putting down his sword he said to Meimei, "I am going for a walk to the waterfall. Would you find Little Li and tell him to join me there? And tell him to come very quietly."

Meimei seldom showed surprise. At the chieftain's words she hesitated only an instant, and then nodded her head. "Very well, sir. I'll find Little Li and tell him to join you at the waterfall."

"And tell him to move quietly," reminded the chieftain.

Having taken this protective measure, the chieftain made his way unhurriedly through the outlaw camp. Most of the villagers were already sleeping, for they were farmers and accustomed to early hours. Once the chieftain heard a child's cry and the soothing voice of its mother. For the most part the camp was quiet, as quiet as could be expected with so many additional people housed in temporary shelters.

Although the chieftain saw no movement and heard no footsteps, he felt himself observed. The ever-vigilant eyes of his enemy were watching him, noting that he was heading for the waterfall. It required a strong effort not to turn his head and look back at the mouth of the cave where his enemy was lurking and watching.

Once again the fine spray from the waterfall chilled him. Already cold with apprehension, he began to shiver from the icy droplets, and soon his teeth were chattering uncontrollably. He began to swing his arms, trying to warm himself and stop his shivering. He wanted to face his enemy with dignity, not trembling like a coward.

Meimei should have given Little Li the message by now. For a moment he wondered how the girl would react to the unmasking of the traitor. Again he was tantalized by her resemblance to someone he knew, and suddenly he saw it: Meimei looked like Wu Meng. Why hadn't he seen it before? The last piece of the puzzle fitted into place.

As a child the chieftain had loved to play a game called Seven Pieces. A set consisting of seven small flat pieces of wood, variously shaped, fitted together in a square box. The pieces could be taken out and used to form many interesting shapes: animals, plants, buildings.

In trying to discover the identity of the phantom in white, the chieftain had a number of clues, like pieces of a puzzle. The first one was the matter of the phantom's costume. How did he change in and out of his white jacket so quickly? This was the easiest question to answer: the phantom simply reversed his jacket and wore the white lining face out. In the outlaw camp all the men wore unlined jackets and were waiting until the weather turned colder before they started wearing lined or padded ones. All but one man.

The second clue was the money box. Given the situation in the hills after that raid, only one man had the opportunity to empty the box. Of course, the governor could have tricked the outlaws with an empty box, but after questioning Suying, he knew the governor had not done so.

The third clue was that the man playing the role of the phantom was a superb actor, the best actor in the camp. There were other good actors, to be sure, but the phantom had to be someone who also knew the story of Zhang Ru. Thinking of the vow of eternal friendship, the chieftain felt bitterness rise like bile in his throat. His tormentor was someone very close to him, and that was his fourth clue.

Meimei had suggested the possibility that the phantom might be the son of Zhang Ru, coming for revenge. But that was ruled out after Fushan Village, when the chieftain had his fifth clue. During the rescue of the villagers, there had been a change of plans, and Little Li had told Gao San to make sure the chieftain got the message. Gao San had told Wu Meng. Nevertheless the chieftain had failed to receive the message and had nearly been killed at the west gate.

Was Wu Meng the phantom in white? The sixth clue lay in the young officer himself. He disagreed with the chieftain in policy, but he was young, handsome, and universally admired. Why should he resort to a shabby ruse to gain control of the leadership? For the chieftain saw clearly that the true mainspring behind the phantom was jealousy. Wu Meng had no reason to be jealous of the chieftain—rather the reverse.

That brought the chieftain to his seventh and final clue, the resemblance between Wu Meng and Meimei. The girl had been serving him for nearly two months, and he was probably the only person in the camp who had not noticed the resemblance. And he was so proud of his power of observation! But he knew the reason for his blindness: he was too preoccupied by the loss of his youth, and whenever he thought of Wu Meng and Meimei, it was always to wonder if the girl might be attracted to the younger man.

Now—now that it was too late—he had finally seen the fatal resemblance. It was the last piece of the puzzle. All the other clues were merely suggestive, not conclusive. With this last clue, he knew positively who the phantom was and why he was jealous.

13

十三

The Real Phantom

From the other side of the waterfall came a shrill giggle. Then a soft, breathy voice said, "Han Baota, my friend, you are feeling pretty pleased with yourself, aren't you? You think the outlaw band must be dazzled by your brilliant leadership, don't you?"

Now that the chieftain was listening for it, he could hear the corroding jealousy in that venomous voice, the jealousy that had been eating away all the original good nature of his enemy.

"You are so busy congratulating yourself that you're forgetting old friends," continued the voice. "You're forgetting old friends and old debts."

The chieftain no longer felt cold. He was warmed by his growing anger. "I have not forgotten Zhang Ru," he said, his voice trembling with a deep anger. "He went mad at the end, but before that he was a true and loyal friend."

The trembling in his voice was interpreted as fear. "You are afraid," said the figure in white, faintly seen behind the water. It moved closer, passing through the thin waterfall. "You abandoned me to the Tartars, and you are trembling at the thought of my revenge."

The chieftain managed to bring his voice under control. "I had to save my men. If he had been sane, Zhang Ru would have done the same."

The figure in white was so close that the chieftain could see the huge black cavities on its face, where the eyes, nose, and mouth should have been. "Take a good look at my face, Han Baota! The result of your desertion!"

The chieftain's outrage spilled over. Thinking of the weeks of mental anguish he had suffered from the cruel charade, he was roused to fury. "You don't have to keep up your pretenses any longer!" he said. "I don't believe for a moment that you're Zhang Ru!"

The approaching figure stopped and stood motionless. Only its white jacket stirred a little from the breeze. "Why not, Han Baota?" it whispered. "Why not?"

"First of all, you can wipe those patches of black ink from your face," the chieftain said contemptuously. "On a dark night the inky patches might look like huge cavities, but the moon is nearly full tonight and I can see the light strike your eyeballs." He didn't admit, of course, that when he had first seen those dark patches he had been sick with horror.

The figure in white stooped and picked up something from the ground. It was a sheathed sword. "Go on," said the voice. "If you don't think I'm Zhang Ru, who am I?"

The chieftain wondered where Little Li was stationing himself—very close, he hoped. "I thought at first Wu Meng was my betrayer," he said, trying not to stare at the sword.

"But he had no reason to be jealous of me, and jealousy is your main reason, *isn't it, Old Wu?*"

For a moment there was silence except for the faint hiss of the waterfall. Then, with a swift slither Old Wu drew his sword. "I wasn't always jealous of you. That was true when we were boys, because your family was rich while mine was poor, and you always had better tutors and could advance faster in the army. But after I got married I was happy at last. I knew your marriage wasn't as successful as mine." He paused. "And then my wife died."

"You were still better off than I was," said the chieftain. "You had a son, a son who would make any father proud. My wife died too, and I had no one left."

"You have Meimei." The words were said quietly, but something in the tone turned the chieftain cold again. "Seeing Meimei in your cave was like seeing my wife there!"

Where was Little Li? Of course he had been instructed to move quietly, but surely he could give some indication of his presence, some small, reassuring rustle.

It was best to keep talking, decided the chieftain. "It wasn't until tonight that I realized Meimei must bear a resemblance to your wife," he said. His anger was gone and he had only pity for his old friend, the old friend who now held a naked sword in his hand.

"How did you guess Meimei looked like my wife?" demanded Old Wu. "You've never seen her."

"I noticed that Wu Meng and Meimei looked alike," said the chieftain. "Wu Meng doesn't look at all like you, and I assume he must take after his mother."

Suddenly Old Wu's voice rose in anguish. "Day and night

I lived with the thought of my wife in your arms, serving you, lying in your bed!"

The chieftain swallowed. "You should have told me. If I had known how you felt about Meimei, I wouldn't have taken her."

"That's not true!" cried Old Wu. "You always took the best! You were always ahead of me!"

Death felt very close to the chieftain. Involuntarily he looked around for Little Li. Surely it was time for him to step out of concealment.

Old Wu laughed. It was his own laugh, not an imitation of Zhang Ru's giggle, but still it held a note of madness. "You're looking for your pet northerner, aren't you? That overgrown puppy, Little Li? I saw him stealing off to Suying's hut. He'll be too busy to be your bodyguard tonight. Nobody will try to stop me from killing you now."

"I will," said a voice, and a tall figure appeared behind Old Wu.

Old Wu's reaction was instantaneous. With a snarl he whipped around and struck.

And his son, who had made no move to defend himself, fell to his knees, clutching his chest. As the two older men watched in horror, Wu Meng reached out a bloody hand and grasped his father's sword arm. "Don't . . . do . . . it," he gasped. Then his hand dropped and he rolled to the ground.

Tears were streaming down Old Wu's cheeks, streaking the ink and making a hideous mask of his face. "Why didn't he tell me who he was?" he moaned. "Why didn't he defend himself?"

The chieftain knew the answer. Wu Meng had offered his life in an attempt to stop his father from committing the unspeakable crime of killing his own general. The chieftain also knew the gesture was futile. He was finding it hard to see clearly, for his own eyes were blurred with tears. Dimly he saw Old Wu turn toward him once more with raised sword. But even as his arms lifted to strike, Old Wu stiffened, opened his eyes wide, and fell forward on his face. Sunk deep in his back was a spear.

Little Li stepped up and bowed abjectly before the chieftain. "I was almost too late, sir. Can you forgive me?"

Meimei appeared behind the young northerner. "He was feeling forlorn and went for a walk. That's why I had trouble finding him."

The chieftain nodded, not interested in Little Li's reasons, guessing only that it had to do with Suying. He walked over to Old Wu and lifted his head. One look at the fixed, staring eyes told him his old friend was dead. Then he turned to Wu Meng and felt the younger man's heart. His hands touched blood, but to his joy he could feel the heart beating.

"Quick, tear up some cloths for bandages!" he said to Meimei. "I think we can save him!"

"Yes, he can receive visitors," Master Feng told the chieftain. "The truth is, the wound is not a grave one, but his spirits are low and that retards his recovery. If you can talk to him and ease his mind a little, I think he will regain his strength more quickly."

Just as the chieftain started for Wu Meng's cave, Master Feng called him back. "I've just thought of something else. You'd better get another woman to take care of him. That woman in there now used to serve his father, and she spends so much time sobbing and making disgusting noises that it's enough to cause a relapse in anyone."

The chieftain nodded. Master Feng might sound sarcastic, but he must have noticed the distress of Old Wu's woman and wanted something done for her. The chieftain blamed himself for not having thought of it sooner. Very well, he would try to make some arrangement. Perhaps there was a widower among the Fushan villagers. . . .

He entered the cave and stood looking down at Wu Meng, who was lying with eyes closed and a quilt drawn up to his neck. At a sign from the chieftain, Old Wu's woman quickly scuttled out. Sighing, the chieftain sat down on a stool and looked at the still, pale face on the bed. Over the years he had watched the ardent boy whom he had loved like a son develop into an ambitious, formidable warrior. As his respect for Wu Meng grew, however, his love had diminished. Some would say he was jealous, but he knew that it was because his ideals and those of Wu Meng were too far apart. And now, because of Old Wu, the breach between them was beyond hope of repair. He sighed again, more deeply, for some of his affection for the younger man still lingered.

Wu Meng opened his eyes. "I'm sorry. If I had acted sooner, none of this would have happened."

"You didn't know," said the chieftain. "He was such a good actor that he fooled us all."

"I should have guessed," said Wu Meng. He grimaced. "Can I have a drink?"

The chieftain found a cup of cold, weak tea on a table beside the bed. Carefully lifting Wu Meng's head, he held the cup to the other man's dry, cracked lips.

Wu Meng drank down the cup eagerly but shook his head when the chieftain offered to make more tea. "I knew my father was obsessed by Meimei," he said, speaking more easily after the drink. "I didn't notice her resemblance to my mother at first because I only remember my mother as sickly and old before her time. One day I overheard two of the women discussing my resemblance to Meimei. I became curious and asked her about her background. There was nothing to indicate that she might be a relative. Then I began to notice that my father stared fixedly at Meimei when he thought he was unobserved."

"That alone was not suspicious," said the chieftain. "It was natural that he should stare at a girl who looked so much like his dead wife."

Wu Meng moved his head restlessly on the pillow. "I discovered that he was spying on your movements, especially at night. At first I thought the two of you went out together to discuss plans for the band, but that didn't explain why he always moved so furtively. I couldn't ask what he was doing, because he no longer confided in me."

To see someone you've loved all your life changing into a stranger, that was a tragic experience, one the chieftain had gone through with Zhang Ru. "What made you follow your father to the waterfall?" he asked.

Wu Meng drew a ragged breath. "I wasn't sure my father actually intended to harm you, not at first. But after our expedition to Fushan Village, I knew. Gao San gave me the message about the change of plans, and I meant to tell you. But shortly afterward we were attacked by a score of soldiers. I wanted to spare my father as much of the fighting as possible, and so I asked him to go and give you the message while I engaged the soldiers. He promised me he would."

"And the message never reached me," the chieftain said softly. Almost to himself he added, "I think that at the end your father went mad, just like Zhang Ru. Before that he was a loyal friend."

Wu Meng nodded, exhausted, and closed his eyes. Looking at his pale face, the chieftain thought that perhaps some of the tension had gone from it.

The chieftain was sitting in his cave hunched over his table when he heard someone approaching softly. "Shall I make some tea for you, sir?" said Meimei's voice.

He nodded and, watching her graceful movements, he realized that because her presence was so quiet and unobtrusive it was easy to take her for granted. Perhaps that had been his mistake, to take her for granted.

"Meimei," he said suddenly, "I was wrong in taking you into my service without consulting your wishes first. If you had your choice, would you rather have been given to Old Wu? Or perhaps to someone young and handsome, like Wu Meng?"

Meimei smiled faintly. "It wasn't a question of handing me to some deserving member of your band. I joined the Tiger Mountain band of my own free will, and my sole aim was to become your consort. That was my choice, and I am content."

"But I don't remember giving you a chance to express a wish in the matter," said the chieftain.

There was genuine amusement in her eyes. "I was not a helpless captive of war, or one of those soft serving women in the mansions of the rich. If I hadn't wanted to be your mistress, I would have found a way to let you know."

"I believe you would," laughed the chieftain. Then he sobered. "Why did you choose me? Because I was the chieftain?"

"I would be lying if I denied it," admitted Meimei. "But also because you possessed qualities I valued: compassion and sagacity."

She was proud, the chieftain realized. A woman like Meimei was not a bolt of silk or a money box taken in a raid. She had gone to him of her own free will. He felt a rush of tenderness for her, and at that moment he decided she deserved to be more than a serving girl. Despite the difference in their ages and her humble origin, she deserved to be his wife.

Little Li and the scribe were sitting in a clearing discussing Wu Meng's intention to leave the outlaw band. Behind them were the yells of children kicking a ball made of pig's bladder.

"I don't see why he has to go away," Little Li said. "Nobody blames him for what his father did. In fact, he tried to save the chieftain's life."

"I don't think he's leaving because of what the others think," said the scribe. "He's going because he differs too much with the chieftain over matters of policy, and as long as he is here, there is a danger of a rift within the band. Don't forget what happened when the chieftain wanted to buy the medicine for Suying. There was a near mutiny here."

Little Li remembered the tension of the camp during that

episode and was forced to agree. But he still felt an aching sense of loss, for Wu Meng was the best fighter in the band, and they were unlikely to find anyone else nearly as good as he was. "And to think that I even suspected him of being the phantom in white?"

"I never suspected him, not for an instant," said the scribe.

"Why not?" demanded Little Li. "Of course it's easy enough for you to say that now."

"Come, come, use your intelligence, if you have any," mocked the scribe. "Cast your mind back to the night when you raided the money box. Wu Meng had sensed that I was following him, and he seized me—with unnecessary force, I might add. After that, we were together. When the money box was tampered with and when the phantom gave his performance, the two of us were in each other's company. How could he be the guilty one?" Having said this, the scribe sat with a smug smile that made Little Li want to hit him.

Which was why Little Li fell back laughing when a ball flew through the air and thumped the scribe on the head. Scowling furiously, the scribe turned to look at a group of grinning village boys. "Why don't you occupy yourselves with something useful?" he asked them.

Still grinning, the boys approached. "There's nothing to do," one of them said. "Back home we'd be helping with the harvest, but here we can play all day."

"There must be something you can do," said the scribe. "I know! Why don't you carry water? Take those pails over there. Each of you can carry a pail of water from the stream."

"We're too small to carry water," piped a little boy of six with no front teeth. "We'll spill it all."

"I'll have to think of something," muttered the scribe. Suddenly he sat up and beamed. "You can learn to read and write!"

"Only the gentry read and write," said the oldest boy. "We're going to be bandits."

"I'm a bandit, and I can read and write," said the scribe. "I'll teach you."

One of the boys was shyer than the rest, and until then he had hung back. Now he stepped forward. "I don't want to write, but I want to learn to draw pictures."

The scribe smiled. "Writing is very much like drawing pictures." He picked up a stick and made scratches on the ground. "Look, this is the word for 'horse.' See its mane and its four legs. And this is the word for 'mountain.' Can you see its three peaks?"

Little Li felt wistful as he left the scribe and his makeshift school. He wanted to learn too, but it would be too mortifying to join a class of little children. Perhaps he could ask the scribe for some private lessons.

After a while he found himself walking toward Wu Meng's cave. Was there any hope of persuading him to stay?

Wu Meng was polishing his sword. He looked up at Little Li's approach and said, "I'm glad you came. I was going to look for you to give you this." He indicated a wooden box.

Little Li lifted the lid and stared at a pile of silver coins. "The money that was supposed to be in the strongbox!"

"He must have hidden the money in the woods and then gone back for it afterward," said Wu Meng. He didn't look up. "I found it among his things under the bed."

"Why did he take the money in the first place?" asked Little Li.

"I suppose to make the raid look like a failure and cast doubt on the chieftain's competence," said Wu Meng. He kept his voice under control, and if it was costing him an effort, he gave no sign of it. "Perhaps he planned to use the money to buy the loyalty of men like Gao San, if the phantom scheme didn't work."

"All right, I'll take the money to the chieftain," Little Li said gruffly. He didn't want to talk any more about Old Wu.

Suddenly Wu Meng looked up. "I'm joining the Imperial Army again, Little Li. Would you like to come with me?"

Little Li's throat tightened and for a moment he could not speak. Then he drew a breath. "The chieftain doesn't think there is any hope of stemming the Tartars. The court is too corrupt to offer resistance."

"But we can still fight on," said Wu Meng. His eyes were bright. "To die defending our country from the barbarians, what could be more glorious for a warrior?"

Wu Meng had been Little Li's ideal. Comparing the other man's dazzling abilities with his own inexperience, Little Li had always felt like a clumsy boy. But now it was Wu Meng who seemed like a boy, a boy whose head was filled with stories of romance and glory.

"I'm sorry," Little Li said, struggling to get the words out. "I can't go with you. There are too many things to do here." He rushed quickly out of the cave, because he could not bear to see the bleak disappointment on Wu Meng's face.

It was true that there were too many things to do in the camp. He saw the scribe scratching in the dirt with his stick, surrounded by a circle of boys. He saw the monk instructing a class of beginners from the village. Master Feng was teaching some women about medicinal herbs. The Pig Woman and her son were putting finishing touches to their pen. Everywhere there was activity.

The barbarians would probably sweep south and conquer the whole of China, just as Wu Meng had said. Here on Tiger Mountain, men and women had a duty not to die gloriously, but to survive. Only outlaw bands like this one, entrenched in the mountains, could offer effective resistance to the conquerors. Someday, if they had the support of the people, they might push out the barbarians and regain their country.

But first they had to live, one day to the next. They had to build shelters, stock food, guard the children. They were more than a band now, they were a community, and there was much to be done.